King of the Vagabonds

'You're still very young,' she said, 'and young enough to heed my advice. So while you're still here with me I give you a warning. Don't go into Quartermile Field. It's a dangerous place. You can go as far as Belinda's meadow. One day, perhaps, you'll go farther. But don't stray into Quartermile Field. I myself have never been there and any animal with sense avoids the spot. Remember what I say.'

Sammy was silent. His tail twitched slightly as he stared at his mother. Her warning had struck home. He was suitably shaken.

Colin Dann

King of
the Vagabonds

RED FOX

A Red Fox Book

Published by Random House Children's Books
20 Vauxhall Bridge Road, London SW1V 2SA

A division of Random House UK Ltd
London Melbourne Sydney Auckland
Johannesburg and agencies throughout the world

Copyright © Colin Dann 1987

1 3 5 7 9 10 8 6 4 2

First published in Great Britain by
Hutchinson Children's Books 1987
Beaver edition 1988

Red Fox edition 1997

Printed and bound by CPI Antony Rowe, Eastbourne

Papers used by Random House UK Limited
are natural, recyclable products made from wood grown in
sustainable forests. The manufacturing processes conform to
the environmental regulations of the country of origin.

RANDOM HOUSE UK Limited Reg. No. 954009

ISBN 0 09 921192 0

Contents

1	The New Kittens	7
2	Climbing	12
3	Learning	17
4	Exploring	25
5	Wondering	33
6	Searching	42
7	The Vagabonds	51
8	Brute	60
9	Exchanges	70
10	A Feast for a Morsel	80
11	New Ways	91
12	Quartermile Field	101
13	Beau	112
14	Sammy's Choice	121
15	The Test Begins	128
16	Survival of the Fittest	139
17	The King Cat	151

For my brother Christopher, with affection

—1—

The New Kittens

It was quite a surprise for Mrs Lambert when her tortoiseshell cat Stella gave birth to a litter of six kittens, for Stella was far from being a young animal. She had recently taken to frequenting the shed at the bottom of the garden, but Mrs Lambert's suspicions had not been aroused since Stella often slept in the shed during the summer when it was too hot in the garden. It was in the shed that Mrs Lambert found Stella and her six tiny kittens, comfortably nestling amongst some old rugs.

'Well, Stella!' cried her mistress in astonishment. 'I thought your kittening days were long over.' She did not know whether to be glad or sorry. However, there was no doubt about Stella's feelings on the matter. She looked at Mrs Lambert with a blissful expression and purred proudly, feeling the fluffy little creatures pressed tight against her.

The kittens appeared to be either tortoiseshells like their mother, or tabbies, which gave a clue to the other half of their parentage. They looked delightful, so tiny and helpless, huddling in their mother's warmth. A shaft of sunlight slanted through the open doorway, lighting up the scene, and Stella blinked contentedly as she looked at her mistress. Mrs Lambert did not dare to disturb them to have a closer look and really she could not think of another cat in the neighbourhood who might be

the father. She hurried off to fetch some clean bedding
and some light nourishment for Stella. Drowsily Stella
licked her kittens. She felt snug and lazy. 'Keep close,
keep close,' she purred.

Mrs Lambert lived alone except for Stella and another
pet, an old mongrel bitch called Molly who looked something like a Labrador, but had a longer coat. Mr Lambert
had died a few years earlier. In the past he had dealt with
the disposal of Stella's litters of kittens and so now his
widow was faced with something of a problem – she knew
that, when these latest ones grew bigger, she would not
be able to afford to feed them all. An idea occurred
to her.

A neighbour's boy sometimes came to do the heavier
gardening jobs which Mrs Lambert could no longer
manage. She was elderly and not very strong and so was
very grateful for his help. She thought it would be a nice
gesture to offer the boy first choice of the kittens to keep
for himself. And there was always the chance that one or
two of his schoolfriends might like a pet as well.

After a couple of weeks the kittens' eyes had opened,
they moved around a little, though very unsteadily, and
mewed a good deal. It soon became clear that some of
them were more attractive than others. One of the tabbies,
in particular, was really unattractive. He had a strange
broad diagonal stripe running across his head that made
his face look as if it had been somehow crossed out. Mrs
Lambert had no hopes of his being chosen by anyone.

Next time the boy came to do some digging, Mrs Lambert took him to the shed. The kittens by then were four
weeks old.

'Look, Edward, what do you think of them?' Mrs Lambert asked him.

Edward was entranced. He loved animals and spent a
long time watching the kittens' antics.

'Would you like one?' offered the old lady.

The boy's eyes shone. 'Yes, please, Mrs Lambert. I'd love one!' he replied, without hesitation.

Mrs Lambert told him that as soon as the kittens could do without their mother, he could come and choose one to take home and, later, he could bring his friends if they were interested. He promised he would ask around at school and was obviously delighted with the whole arrangement.

Poor Stella was very tired and seemed at times a little bewildered by the situation that had developed. The kittens' demands were exhausting her, despite the extra nourishment her mistress was now providing. Mrs Lambert was relieved when the time at last arrived for Edward to make his selection. She told him that the tortoiseshells were all female and the tabbies all male and left him alone with them. He took quite a while to decide but, in the end, plumped for a tortoiseshell because, as he said, 'I'd like mine to have some kittens one day.'

About a week afterwards he brought three of his friends along. They all declared they wanted males but, when they saw how ugly one of the three tabby kittens was, it seemed that the only way out was for one child to have a female. There was a bit of difficulty but eventually everything was sorted out quite amicably and they all went away as pleased as Punch with their new pets. So Mrs Lambert was left with the ugly tabby and one tortoiseshell. She had already made up her mind to keep one kitten and, since she did not have the heart to dispose of the tabby in any unpleasant way, she was content to keep him as well. She called him Sammy and his sister Josephine.

Stella soon recovered her strength and began to show her remaining youngsters around her mistress's garden and cottage to familiarize them with their immediate surroundings. The old bitch Molly showed a great interest in the little animals and they were soon fast friends and all playing together.

Sammy and Josephine loved to chase each other up and down the garden and they teased their mother and Molly unmercifully, pouncing on them from behind plants and seizing hold of their tails. The older animals were very tolerant of their games, but the kittens soon learnt just how far they could go with Stella. She was prepared to put up with just so much biting from sharp little teeth and no more.

The kittens grew quickly and Mrs Lambert noticed that Sammy was inclined to be more adventurous and inquisitive than his sister. It was not long before he had climbed the fence round her garden, though he was not confident enough yet to venture outside it.

The kittens loved Mrs Lambert, and she was very kind to them. She allowed them into the cottage whenever they wished, though they still looked upon the shed as their real home. They would follow her tall, grey-haired, rather bony figure from room to room. Indeed she had to be careful: she had rather an awkward gait, brought on by years of rheumatism, and they would sometimes get right under her feet. She was afraid of treading on them, especially Sammy who was the more lively and energetic of the two.

Both the kittens soon learned to answer to their own names, and also to understand when their mistress was calling Stella or Molly instead. Their mother was always reminding them of how fortunate they all were.

'We're very lucky,' she would say. 'We have such a kind mistress who looks after us all so well.'

They became accustomed to hearing such phrases and so an awareness formed in their minds of the little family of which they were a part and they felt very comfortable.

Every morning Mrs Lambert let Molly out into the garden. The dog would waddle straight over to the shed, wagging her tail feebly as she went, to see if the kittens were there. If they were missing she would begin a search of the garden which usually resulted in her being pounced on from some corner unexpectedly. The gentle old animal would yelp in delight and, as the kittens raced off again, she would make vain attempts to catch them. Mrs Lambert chuckled a lot at these games.

Eventually the youngsters would quieten down. Josephine returned to her mother whilst Sammy would rub himself round Molly, his little tail stuck up straight in the air as he purred out his friendship.

Molly's first remark was always the same. 'How you grow! You'll soon be as big as your mother.'

One day Sammy answered, 'Perhaps I'll be bigger–like my father.' He had started to dream about his father since he had learnt there was such a creature. He imagined him to be strong and clever although, of course, he had never seen him and knew next to nothing about him. Stella had told him very little.

Molly, who had been around for a long time, had a shrewd suspicion who was the father of the kittens.

'Yes, you may grow to be like your father,' she said. 'But his sort of life is not for you. How lucky *you* are to have a proper home.'

Sammy knew he was lucky because Stella was always telling him so. But Molly's remarks only made him more curious about his father.

—2—

Climbing

Sammy began to stray farther from his mother, and Stella made no attempt to stop him. In the middle of Mrs Lambert's lawn was an ancient gnarled apple tree with broad spreading branches just begging to be climbed. Sammy could not resist its call. He hauled himself easily up the trunk, his claws digging deep into the crusty bark. He found that he could walk along a main branch and look out across the whole garden. He could see Stella and Josephine basking in the sun. He could see Mrs Lambert pottering about in her kitchen. And he could see farther – out over the neighbouring gardens to some open land beyond. He climbed higher for a better view. Now he could see more. The open land was dotted with the ruins of human habitations. There had been houses here but they had been destroyed in the war and no rebuilding had taken place since on the site. Beyond that, fields and trees stretched as far as the eye could reach. But what interested Sammy was certain movements amongst the tall weeds on the bomb site. There were animals there and he was sure they were cats. He wanted to find out. It seemed there was a lot more than just his mistress's garden to explore.

The leaves of the apple tree rustled above his head. He saw Molly waddle underneath its boughs and heard her whine. She was looking up at him with a worried expression on her grizzled old face.

'I'm all right,' Sammy called down to her reassuringly. 'Climbing is easy.'

'It may be,' was Molly's answer. 'But what about coming down?'

Sammy had not thought much about that. 'Oh, it won't be any bother,' he told her, but with rather less confidence. He turned round carefully on the branch. That was easy enough. Then he looked down to the larger branch he had first got on to. He was not quite certain how he was going to return to that. Should he go forwards or – or – backwards? This was not so simple after all. Perhaps he could jump from one branch to another. But supposing he should miss his footing? He looked down, trying to assess whether he could manage such a large leap. His body dipped up and down as he attempted to gauge the risk.

Molly could tell Sammy was in difficulty. She set off to fetch Stella. Sammy's mother received the news with equanimity.

'It's natural for him to want to test his skills,' she commented. 'All youngsters are the same. He'll manage. He must learn the hard way.'

Just then there came the sound of a crash. The leaves of the apple tree shook vigorously. Sammy had tried his jump.

He had been lucky. He had not landed well on the larger branch and had very nearly overbalanced. Only by sinking his claws really hard into the wood had he managed not to slip right over. But now, having heard the crash, Stella, Molly and Josephine came running.

'He wanted to climb the tree. Now he can't get down,' wailed Josephine unhelpfully.

'He *will* get down,' Stella answered her firmly.

However, Sammy, who had reached the lower branch by a whisker, still faced the problem of descending the trunk. He saw his mother and sister watching him as well as Molly, and the temptation to beg Stella for help was almost overwhelming. But he felt he would be demeaning himself in the eyes of the onlookers if he did so. He began to inch his way forward slowly, head first.

'You're too high up to come down that way,' his mother called. 'Swing round and lower yourself by your back legs first.'

Sammy gulped. She sounded so far away. Oh, why had he climbed the wretched tree? It was so much more difficult than a fence.

'Can't you climb up and lead him down, Stella?' Molly asked. 'You could show him how.'

'Of course I could,' she replied. 'But I'm not going to. That's the easy way.'

'Well, I wish I could help,' Molly muttered. '*I* wouldn't abandon him.'

'I'm not abandoning him,' Stella said crossly. 'Sammy has to learn. I won't always be around to rescue him.'

Josephine began to mew to her brother encouragingly, while Stella coolly repeated her directions to him. Somehow Sammy found the courage to swing himself round on the trunk, his claws grappling for a good grip. Then, miaowing nervously at intervals, he crept backwards down to the ground.

'Now, Sammy. You'll know another time,' was all Stella said.

Molly wagged her tail furiously and licked the little tabby's crossed-out face all over in her relief. Josephine rubbed herself against her brother gladly.

When Sammy had fully recovered himself, he started

to ask the older animals questions about what he had seen from the tree top.

'Plenty of time for all that,' Molly counselled. 'One step at a time, you know.'

'Quite right,' said Stella. 'There's a lot you have to know. But not just yet.'

Sammy's curiosity was whetted further by these mysterious remarks, but he knew he would have to try to be patient. His mother had begun to wash herself, and it was clear that he would get no more information from her for the moment.

With the climbing of the tree behind him, Sammy felt very pleased with himself. He was flushed with his success and decided he would soon be ready for new adventures.

Mrs Lambert's neighbour kept chickens. Sammy had watched them scratching about in their wire enclosure from the fence top. His opinion of the hens was that they were rather silly creatures who always seemed to be making a song and dance over nothing in particular; but he had been impressed by one bird who was different from the others and who appeared to be in charge. Though he did not realize it, this was the cockerel – a very gaudy fellow. He strutted around, lording it over his companions. Sammy was a little in awe of him.

A few days after his first ascent of the apple tree, Sammy was sitting on top of the fence admiring the self-important cockerel. He stepped sedately up and down, pausing now and then to crow. Sammy took this to be some sort of challenge and jumped into the neighbour's garden.

At once the hens began to run about, clucking nervously. But the cockerel behaved in a different way. He turned his bright eyes on Sammy and made threatening noises. Sammy looked back at the fierce cockerel, but was not deterred. He began to climb up the wire netting of the hen run.

The cockerel made a quick dash towards him. 'See what you're doing!' he cried. 'Look at my hens! Oh, if you want to cause mischief—' He left the remainder of the implied threat in the air.

Sammy paused. The cockerel looked to be ready for action and he did seem a bird not to be trifled with. The young cat climbed back down the netting, returning to the ground.

'I'm not mischievous,' he said to mollify the cockerel. 'But I *can* climb!' The knowledge of this was Sammy's great pride.

'Climb! But can you fly?' retorted the cockerel, who had been deprived of this ability, and was therefore all the more impressed by it.

'Don't be silly,' said Sammy. 'I'm a cat, not a bird.'

'Well, when you can do something as clever as flying, you may come and tell me,' was the cockerel's answer. 'Otherwise – don't bother us.'

Sammy was deflated. He thought he *had* been clever. But the cockerel's remark made him think. All cats climbed   so what was so special about what he had done? The apple tree lost its significance. He started to wander away but the squawking of the hens had aroused their owner who now appeared in the garden to chase the intruder away. Sammy made a hasty exit. The man's shouts frightened him and he was glad to scramble over the fence and rejoin his friends.

After this Sammy kept himself quiet for a while. He grew steadily and he did not forget what he had seen from the apple tree.

—3—

Learning

The trouble was, life was too quiet. Stella and Josephine were quite content to stay in their own garden. As Josephine got bigger, she became more and more like her mother, in looks and in temperament. She was docile, almost to the point of serenity. They spent most of their time together and resembled two sisters rather than mother and daughter. Sammy was not resentful of their preference for each other's company. He enjoyed a feeling of freedom and, in any case, there was always Molly.

Sammy was very fond of Molly. She seemed to understand him and, although at her age she was not the most exciting of animals, she had a great fund of knowledge about all sorts of things. In her younger days she had accompanied her master far and wide in the area. She knew all about what went on at the bomb site; what creatures were there and how they lived. But she was always careful not to make the outside world sound attractive to Sammy. In fact she warned him of what life could be like for those who were less fortunate than themselves. She wanted to be sure the young cat did not harbour any ideas of trying out his father's sort of existence, for she soon noticed he was very interested in him. He was always wondering what he looked like and if he would ever see him.

At night Sammy, Stella and Josephine usually slept in the shed which always remained open. It was warm and dry and they had it all to themselves, except for the occasional mouse. But, since they were so comfortable and well fed, none of them showed any interest in mice. Stella had never been known to catch one and so the two youngsters were equally indifferent.

One night Sammy lay awake while the other cats slept. He felt restless and was thinking of his father again. There was a pitter-patter of quick little feet across the shed floor. Bright moonlight penetrated the wooden building and Sammy looked around him listlessly. A mouse was running about in search of titbits. Sammy watched with no more than a flicker of interest.

The mouse stopped, sat on its hind legs and wrinkled its nose. Its forepaws hung limp as it tested the air. Some sixth sense had told the little animal it was noticed.

'I know you're watching me,' the mouse squeaked. 'I shall see you in a moment.' It made no move to run away, perhaps because it was not sure which was the safest direction to run.

'I *am* watching,' Sammy confessed, 'but for no special reason.'

The mouse dropped to all fours and his little black beady eyes focussed on the cat. When he was sure who had spoken he relaxed visibly.

'Sammy,' he said.

'Yes,' said the cat. 'How do you know?'

'I've watched you grow up, you and your sister. I was born in the shed too.' And the mouse squeaked with amusement.

'I don't know your name,' Sammy said. He was wide awake now and becoming more interested.

'Tiptoe.'

'Very appropriate, I should think. Anyway, it's good to

see a new face. Nothing ever happens around here.'

'You've got to make it happen,' the mouse told him. 'I get into no end of scrapes. The other day I climbed up the shed door. Just as I got to the top a gust of wind caught it and blew it back against the wall. I just had time to jump down or I should have been squashed flat.'

'That was a huge jump for a little creature like you,' said Sammy.

'An *enormous* jump,' Tiptoe averred. 'But cats aren't the only animals who can jump. Of course, I was a bit shaken up for a while, so I went and found something to eat and then I soon felt better.'

'Doesn't the mistress feed you?' Sammy asked naively.

'The mistress? Oh, you mean – no, no, she doesn't know about us mice. At least, I hope she doesn't. Human beings don't approve of us usually. Tee hee hee.' He seemed to find it all very comical.

Sammy was delighted with his new friend. He seemed to have more life in his tiny body than Stella, Molly and Josephine rolled into one.

'Ours is a very kind mistress,' Sammy informed Tiptoe loyally.

'So I understand,' came the reply, 'and she's been kind to me more than once, only she doesn't know it. Tee hee.'

'How?'

'Oh, I often find scraps you cats or the dog have dropped or left behind. And then there's your mistress's own scraps too. We mice never go short, you know.'

'I can see that,' Sammy remarked. 'But, you know, you're very welcome to some of my food. I always have more than enough. You don't have to wait for the scraps.'

'Well, that's a new notion, certainly,' the mouse replied. 'I suppose I should be grateful although, to be honest, I prefer my way of foraging around. That way, you never quite know what you may find. And then, a lot of what *you* eat doesn't appeal to me at all.'

'You're very independent,' said Sammy. He was comparing Tiptoe's way of life with his own. The idea of actually having to look around for food had never entered his head.

'Have to be, don't I?' Tiptoe laughed good-naturedly.

'You remind me of my father,' Sammy murmured.

'Your father?' Tiptoe cried. 'Why, was he a mouse?'

Sammy chuckled. 'Of course not. But I believe he has to catch his own food.'

'Cats of that sort don't recommend themselves to me at all,' replied the mouse. 'Woe betide small creatures who cross their path. But I don't remember seeing a grown male cat around?'

'He's not around,' declared Sammy. 'I don't know where he is.'

'Oh, I follow,' Tiptoe muttered to himself. 'One of the wandering sort.'

'What?' asked Sammy, who did not understand.

Just then Stella stirred and they were interrupted. Tiptoe decided discretion was the better part of valour and scuttled away. Before he was quite out of earshot, Sammy begged him to come again and renew their friendship.

'I will,' squeaked Tiptoe. 'Just when you least expect it. Tee hee!'

'Sammy?' It was Stella's voice.

'Yes, I'm here.'

'Were you talking?'

'Er – sort of. Mother, is my father a wandering sort of cat?'

'Well now, I wonder what put that idea into your head,' said Stella.

'Because I've never seen him round here,' Sammy said. Naturally he was not going to mention Tiptoe.

'Why are you so concerned about him?' she returned. 'Josephine never asks.' But there was just a suggestion of a wistful note in her voice which Sammy immediately detected.

'I want to know what he's like,' he said eagerly. 'Will I ever see him?'

'You may – and you may not,' Stella replied evasively. 'I can't tell. He hasn't come this way for a long time.'

'Oh, you're just like Molly,' Sammy wailed in exasperation. 'She never gives anything away about him, and I'm sure she knows.'

Stella had heard from Molly that Sammy was forever questioning her. She considered for a moment. She realized that the youngster was entitled to know some things about his father.

'All right,' she said. 'Let's sleep now. But I promise that tomorrow I'll tell you a little about him.'

That made the excited Sammy even less inclined to sleep but he knew he had to be content for the time being.

The next morning he, Stella and Josephine lay in the shade underneath the apple tree. It was very warm. Mrs Lambert had given them milk and they were feeling refreshed and comfortable. Molly was lying on her side a little distance off on the grass, enjoying the full effect of the sun's rays on her old bones. Sammy waited for his mother to keep her promise. At length she began.

'You were asking if you would ever see your father. I can't tell you, because his movements are very unpredictable. He makes an appearance quite unexpectedly and then, just as suddenly, he'll depart. And no one will know where he's going.'

Molly's ears had pricked up. She had been eaves-
dropping. Now she raised her head and called out: 'If
your father is who I think he is, Sammy, it would be better
if you never did see him. A wilder sort of creature *I've*
never come across.'

A strange look came over Stella and, to Sammy's surprise, she became rather defensive. 'Oh, not so wild,
Molly,' she said. 'I know him better than you.'

Molly was unperturbed. She waddled over. 'Well, he
always seemed to have come from some scrap or other
whenever I saw him,' she maintained.

Sammy was enthralled and even Josephine started to
show some interest.

'Naturally he has to defend himself,' Stella answered
the dog.

'What is his name?' murmured Sammy.

'I've always known him as Beau,' his mother said.

'Beau,' Sammy repeated. He liked the sound of it.
'Beau, Beau,' he chanted.

'Now you know, and a lot of good it will do you,' Molly
said to him.

'It will do him no harm to know his father's name,'
Stella asserted.

'Is he a fierce cat?' Josephine wanted to know.

'He's never been fierce with me,' Stella answered. 'But
he has to look after himself and there may be one or two
other male cats around who might have a different idea
of him.'

Sammy was so excited he could not keep still.
Josephine, though, thought it was sad. 'Why doesn't he
have a mistress to feed him?' she asked innocently.

'He doesn't need one,' Sammy answered quickly. His
head was full of wonderful new ideas about this unknown
animal.

'He feeds himself,' Stella explained to Josephine. 'But,

let me tell you both, that's no substitute for having a kind mistress to look after you and see you never want for anything.'

'No, indeed,' Molly agreed. 'And if your father was here now you'd see what we mean.'

This was Sammy's dearest wish. 'Oh, if only he *would* come,' he said. 'But tell us more about him. Please.'

Now that the subject of Beau was fully out in the open, Stella did not seem at all loth to discuss him. 'Well then, he's a tabby like you, Sammy. But then again, he's not really like you at all. His coat is darker and duller – not glossy like yours. He's a big animal but lean and hard and muscular. And when he walks he looks straight ahead in a very determined sort of way. His voice is harsh and his eyes are a glittering green that seem to pierce right through you.'

Sammy was enraptured. Josephine was not. She was even a little frightened. 'He sounds horrible to me,' she mewed.

'He's only hard because he's had a hard life,' Stella soothed her. 'It's hard finding enough food; hard finding shelter when it's cold or wet; hard defending himself against others—'

'A hateful existence,' put in Molly.

'How tremendous,' whispered Sammy. The adults did not hear and this was just as well because the young cat was vowing to himself he would try to emulate this wonderful creature, his father, in every way he could. However, just as he was trying with all his might to pierce his sister with a fierce look from his own eyes, Mrs Lambert appeared from the cottage and he found himself being swung unceremoniously into the air for a cuddle.

Fond as Sammy was of his gentle mistress, a more inappropriate time could not have been chosen for her caresses. He was still thinking of Beau and now he tried to behave like him. He struggled in Mrs Lambert's arms, actually unsheathing his claws to her great astonishment and giving her a scratch or two. Sammy was dumped hurriedly on the ground and given a scolding, but he ran away to the other end of the garden. His feelings were torn between hurt pride and shame at what he had done.

'Sammy seems to have a bit of his father in him,' Molly remarked to Stella when Mrs Lambert had gone back indoors.

'I don't know,' Stella returned. 'Perhaps he has. But I don't see why he should have behaved like that.'

'I think I do,' said Josephine.

—4—

Exploring

Over the next few days Sammy practised his new role. He wandered all over the garden and always tried to walk with his eyes looking straight ahead in a purposeful manner, ignoring all distractions. When he was not sure of something he imagined to himself how his father would react and then carried on accordingly. He used the apple tree every day as his scratching post. His ambition, he had decided, was to find his father, and he intended to do so, by his own efforts if necessary, as soon as he was full grown. Meanwhile he continued to pump Molly for information about what he had seen from the apple tree, beyond his immediate surroundings. The dog was as cautious as ever about what she told him.

'There are fields and trees mostly, and then more fields and trees. But I've told you all this before.'

'Did you ever see my father around that area, Molly? You know, when you were walking with your master.'

'I'm not sure,' she would say. 'I'm very old now. It's difficult for me to remember.'

Sammy became artful. 'How did you know who my father is if you pretend not to remember anything about him?' he asked her once.

Molly was flummoxed. 'Er – well, I didn't *know*,' she mumbled. 'I guessed.'

'Well, you remember lots of other things perfectly well,' Sammy persisted.

'Oh yes,' she admitted. 'And the thing I remember best of all is how glad I always was, after an outing, to come back here to the warmth and security of my master's home.'

Sammy understood this but was well aware that Molly was trying to put him off. He made such a nuisance of himself that she had to think of something to tell him just to keep him quiet. She said she thought she might have seen Beau once by the stream where Mr Lambert sometimes went fishing. Sammy had no idea what a stream was, and so this topic kept him busy for quite a while.

About a week later Tiptoe turned up again, this time in a very different spot. Mrs Lambert usually fed the three cats and Molly together by the kitchen door. If the weather was bad they ate in the kitchen itself. One day they had all finished their meal and the older animals were preparing for a snooze outside. Josephine invariably followed her mother but Sammy was not in the least inclined to sleep. He stood, looking vacantly into Mrs Lambert's kitchen. Suddenly a slight movement attracted his attention. A tiny brown head emerged, whiskers first, from beneath her refrigerator.

'Hello!' squeaked Tiptoe cheekily as soon as he saw he was spotted. But Mrs Lambert was still about and Sammy watched with amusement as the mouse quickly ducked away again out of sight. He waited, hoping his mistress would move away. The next thing he knew, Tiptoe had scurried out of the door and straight into a clump of alyssum that grew near the cottage wall. It was all so quick that only Sammy noticed. He stepped closer to the plant.

'Fast-footed, aren't I? Tee hee!' came a shrill voice from the midst of the vegetation.

Sammy could not see where the mouse was. He was quite hidden. He looked round to see if any of the other animals were watching, but none of them was paying any attention.

'Had any adventures?' cried Tiptoe.

'Er – no. Have you?'

'Plenty. This could become one now if one of those animals wakes up. Tee-hee!'

'Come down to my shed,' Sammy offered. 'We can talk safely there.' And he walked off, unhurriedly to avoid suspicion, taking care, of course, to look straight ahead.

Sammy had to wait awhile in the dim interior of the shed. But eventually Tiptoe scurried in, having made the journey in fits and starts. Sammy was bursting to tell the mouse of his plan. 'I'm going in search of my father,' he announced proudly.

'Are you? When?'

'When I'm full grown.'

'That's a long way off, isn't it?' asked Tiptoe. 'Are there to be no adventures till then?'

'I don't know. I hadn't thought,' Sammy answered lamely.

'Haven't you done any exploring at all?'

'Of course I have,' Sammy asserted defensively. 'I've been next door and frightened the chickens.'

'And . . . ?'

'Well, nothing else, really.'

'No farther than that?' squeaked Tiptoe in amazement. 'Why, I'm a fraction of your size and I get around much more.'

'Yes, but your size enables you to go where I can't,' Sammy pointed out. 'You can get in and out of places that—'

'Excuses, excuses,' Tiptoe butted in. 'You're excusing yourself.'

'I suppose I am,' the young cat admitted. I'm acting pretty tame, he thought to himself. What has happened to my ambition to imitate my father? He looked at Tiptoe and realized at once that this was something his father would never do. Cat talking to mouse. It was absurd. But then, he liked Tiptoe. He did not have to do *everything* the same as his father.

'You're thinking hard,' observed the mouse.

'Yes. I'm thinking where to explore next,' Sammy lied.

'Good. Well, I'm on my travels again myself now,' said Tiptoe. 'So let's meet here tonight and compare notes.' And in a trice he was gone – as quickly as he had come.

Sammy felt he must do something. He did not wish to be humiliated by a mouse. He pondered awhile. Then he set off.

He climbed the fence on the other side of the garden, away from the neighbouring chickens. There seemed to be nothing but houses and gardens on that side, as far as you could see. It didn't look very interesting, he decided. So he climbed down and went back across the garden to the opposite fence, up and over it, past the chicken run without so much as a sideways glance and on across the neighbour's garden to the next fence. From here he could see a couple more gardens and then, beyond them, a kind of paddock. At the end of that was a road and, across the road, the waste ground. Sammy was becoming excited. He wondered how far he dared go. He went across the next two gardens without hindrance and into the paddock before he could think too much about it. He was pleased with his new purposefulness.

The grass was long and thick in the paddock, which seemed at first sight to be empty. Sammy eased his way through the thick grass to a smoother spot. He looked about him. Now he could see the paddock did have an occupant. It was a large animal, taller but not so stocky as Molly. In fact it was nothing like a dog at all. It was white and its long hair looked clean and silky. It had a bony sort of head, a long neck and a short cropped tail. It was busy tearing at the grass with its teeth and looked docile enough.

However, Sammy was not sure how he would be received by this much larger animal and so he crept forward cautiously. The animal looked up. It was chewing contentedly and did not seem at all surprised at the cat's approach. Sammy held his tail aloft in a polite way and mewed a greeting.

'Haven't seen you before,' the beast bleated at him.

'No. Er – I'm a cat,' Sammy said hesitantly.

'I know you're a cat,' came the reply. 'I'm not daft.'

'Excuse me, but – um – what are you? Not a dog, I think?'

'Hah!' scoffed the animal. 'A dog indeed. I should hope I'm not. Haven't you ever seen a goat before?'

'Actually, I haven't,' said Sammy.

'Ah well, you're still young. Where do you come from?'

'I'm one of Stella's kittens,' Sammy said naïvely. 'I'm Sammy.'

'Are you indeed?' responded the goat with a toss of her head. 'I know Stella. She's been around a long while. D'you find my meadow of interest?'

'I'm just – exploring,' Sammy explained. 'I've hardly been out of the garden before. But there's not much of interest *there*.'

'Well, I don't think you'll find much excitement here,'

the goat remarked. 'Nothing ever happens. That's how I like it.'

'It's very quiet, isn't it?' said Sammy. 'Don't you ever see other animals here?'

'Not often. A hedgehog or two. The occasional cat.' The goat looked at him slyly. 'Your mother used to come here sometimes, when she was feeling a bit frisky, I suppose.'

Sammy had never seen Stella in a frisky mood. He did not understand what the goat meant.

'Only Stella? No other cats?' he asked hopefully.

'Well yes. That's what I was telling you about – when your mother came looking for company. Oh, I expect you're too young to know anything about it.'

'Of course I'm not too young,' Sammy declared, although he had no idea what the goat was talking about. All he wanted to know about was the other cats. 'Was one of the cats a tabby like me?' he persisted.

'You're full of questions, aren't you?' returned the goat. 'There was only one cat that came. *He* was a tabby, yes. A battle-scarred looking animal. But Stella didn't seem to mind that—' She broke off. 'I don't know why I'm telling you this,' she added uncertainly.

'He's my father. Beau,' Sammy asserted proudly.

'Of course, yes. I see it now.'

The young cat looked carefully at the goat to see if he dare risk one more question. She appeared good-humoured enough and she had very gentle eyes.

'I don't know your name,' he mumbled, suddenly abashed.

'Belinda.'

'Do you know, please – er – Belinda, where my father came from?' he asked.

'No, no. How could *I* tell you? I never leave the meadow.'

'Oh.' Sammy could see there was no more information to be gained. It was time to turn back. He had not the courage yet to cross the road. 'I'm sorry to have intruded without your permission,' he said politely. 'I'll leave you in peace.'

'Don't mind me, young tabby,' Belinda told him. 'You don't need to ask first. Just come. I'll be glad to see you. I've known Stella for years, and next time, bring her with you. I've not seen her in a long while.'

'How kind you are,' Sammy answered warmly. 'My mother has been busy with us kittens,' he went on. 'But, as you see, we've become more independent now.'

He hastened back to tell Stella of his new friend. He was fully occupied with his thoughts and was not being very careful. One of the gardens on his homeward route had a dog in it now. The first Sammy knew of it was its sudden furious yapping. He was moving nonchalantly across the grass, looking straight ahead to the next fence. He turned in alarm and saw a small, wire-haired terrier racing towards him on its stubby little legs. It was not much bigger than Sammy but its barks were terrific. Greatly frightened, Sammy broke into a run. The dog put on a spurt, dashing between the cat and the fence, its hackles up and its teeth bared.

Sammy turned tail and fled back to the fence he had just crossed. Swiftly he scrambled up it and sat in safety on the top, his heart pounding furiously and his breathing coming quickly. Now the terrier barred his way home. It stood below, snarling deep in its throat.

The two animals stared at each other. Sammy wondered how he could get back. He had to cross this garden: there was no other way home. The dog seemed content to stay where it was indefinitely, determined to prevent him from passing. There was no human being anywhere about to call it off. Sammy tried to think what his father would do, but the dog's threatening snarls did not help his concentration.

Then he had an idea. He climbed down from the fence into the adjacent garden, pretending he was going away. For a while he crouched amongst some plants, keeping perfectly still. Then, when he thought he had waited long enough, he returned to the fence top. As he had suspected, the terrier had lost interest and wandered off, thinking Sammy had given up. Without hesitation, Sammy jumped down and streaked across. He was up and over the next fence before the terrier had come to its senses.

Sammy was thrilled at having outwitted the dog. Here was an adventure to regale Tiptoe with that night. He reached home without further difficulty, feeling especially pleased with himself.

—5—

Wondering

At night in the shed Sammy told his mother about Belinda and what she had said to him.

'You went as far as that, did you?' Stella remarked, sounding surprised. 'Well, I'm glad you didn't go any farther. It might have been dangerous.'

Sammy thought she was referring to the road. 'Belinda wants you to come with me next time,' he told her. 'She said you used to meet our father there.'

Stella enjoyed an inward smile. It was obvious Sammy did not understand what he was talking about.

Then the young cat began his questions again. Where did Beau come from? Would he come back? When had she last seen him?

'Oh, Sammy. Always the same thing,' Stella sighed.

'I wish we'd never heard of Beau,' Josephine yawned contemptuously.

But Stella would not accept that. 'He *is* your father, Josephine. Don't talk like that. It's only fair that Sammy – and you – should know something about him.' She seemed to be about to tell them. Sammy was agog.

'Your father,' Stella went on, 'comes from – oh! a long way from here. He was born in the open air, under a bush. That was the only shelter his mother could give her family, so he told me. He was brought up and lived amongst a colony of strays, always in the open with no real home. There was a lot of rivalry amongst the males in the group and eventually Beau wandered away to a new area until he grew bigger and stronger. He's been a bit of a wanderer ever since. But he does return from time to time, Sammy, to his favourite haunts.'

'When will he come? When will he come?' Sammy cried excitedly.

'That I can't tell you,' Stella said, 'so it's no use your getting in a state. There's no set pattern to your father's movements and only he could tell you of his plans. Perhaps he *won't* come near here again. I don't know. But I hope—' She broke off and looked away. She was lost in her own private thoughts.

Sammy was exasperated by the uncertainty of his father's re-appearance. Without thinking he blurted out: 'Where would I go to look for him?'

Stella looked at him for a long time before replying. She was evidently searching for the right thing to say.

'Sammy,' she began slowly, 'it would be very foolish of you to set off on such a venture. You have no idea what you might encounter; you don't understand that you'd find things quite different from what we're all used to here.'

She paused. Then she resumed, 'And, to answer your question, I don't know where you would go. You might search high and low and never find Beau. Then again, he might be in the next field. That's how he is.'

Sammy was not at all put off by his mother's words. He had not really been expecting a straightforward answer. What he had been looking for was some sort of clue. As for Stella, she sensed that the young male cat's mind was made up. It would only be a matter of time before he would take it into his head to go off on his search. She understood that there was bound to be a wanderlust in his blood with Beau for a father. She could not prevent his going, but she could try to delay it until he would be better able to cope. There was only one way she could think of doing that – by frightening him. She spoke to Sammy again.

'You're still very young,' she said, 'and young enough to heed my advice. So while you're still here with me I give you a warning. Don't go into Quartermile Field. It's a dangerous place. You can go as far as Belinda's meadow. One day, perhaps, you'll go farther. But don't stray into Quartermile Field. I myself have never been there and any animal with sense avoids the spot. Remember what I say.'

Sammy was silent. His tail twitched slightly as he stared at his mother. Her warning had struck home. He was suitably shaken.

Josephine's flesh crawled. The name of the place seemed to have a sinister ring about it. She said the name over to herself. 'Quartermile Field.' She shivered slightly at the sound of the words.

'Wh – what is it?' Sammy stammered.

'I told you. A very dangerous place,' Stella answered. 'Don't ask me more. I've said enough.'

Sammy thought he would ask Molly about it. But suddenly his desire to search for his father did not seem so urgent after all. It was a long time before either he or Josephine slept. He had forgotten all about the rendezvous with Tiptoe.

The mouse had not. But he did not go far into the shed. The tension created by Stella's warning hung in the close air like a cloud. His fur prickled and he backed away. His instinct told him to run.

The next day the garden appeared to Sammy to be more inviting than it had been for a long time. He ran about, in and out of the plants, and even played with Josephine for a bit. Then he had the idea of climbing the apple tree again to see if he could catch a glimpse of the place whose name was still ringing in his head.

Sammy was a good climber by this time. He had never forgotten his first lesson. From the top of the tree he looked out with more purpose than before at the neighbouring terrain. But, try as he might, he could make out nothing unusual in any of the fields he could see, from the wasteland onwards, though he strained to look farther than ever. He wondered just how far away Quartermile Field could be. Was he looking at it now or was it away, over the horizon? He merely wanted to see it. He certainly meant never to go there.

Eventually he climbed down and went in search of Molly. Perhaps she could help. After all, it could surely do no harm just to know what the place looked like.

The old dog was indoors. The kitchen door, as usual, was open. Sammy stepped into the cottage. Mrs Lambert was in her kitchen, chopping vegetables. She stooped down stiffly to stroke her young cat, speaking to him with affection. This time Sammy returned her affection gladly, rubbing himself around the old lady's legs and miaowing prettily in answer to her remarks. Molly was lying under the table, trying to keep cool.

When Mrs Lambert was busy again, Sammy joined his friend. Molly thumped her tail once or twice in a feeble greeting.

'Can't seem to feel comfortable,' she muttered. 'The heat's awful.'

'It's cooler in the shed,' Sammy suggested.

'Maybe. But I've got to cross the garden to get there.'

'There's something I want to ask you,' said Sammy.

'There always is,' sighed Molly.

Mrs Lambert was listening with amusement to the

animal noises coming from under the table. Presently she peered down in an effort to see what all the fuss was about.

'The mistress is looking at us,' said Sammy.

Molly got to her feet reluctantly and stretched. Sammy took this as a sign that she was ready to follow him. He led her off along the lawn to the shed, and once inside, he burst straight out with his question, without any pre-amble. 'What does Quartermile Field look like Molly? Tell me, please?'

Molly was taken aback. 'How do you know about that?' she asked sharply.

'My mother told me. She warned me never to go there.'

'Of course she did.'

'So you see, I'm curious about it.'

'Best not to be, Sammy. Curiosity killed the cat.'

'But I don't want to go there. I only wondered what it looks like.'

'Oh – it's a field of sorts,' Molly answered vaguely. 'Not unlike the others, until you get into it.'

'Have *you* been into it?' Sammy asked in a breathless voice.

Molly had been into it with her master, but she thought it wise not to admit it. 'It's out of bounds,' she answered bluntly.

Sammy was disappointed. Molly was always so obscure.

Then, surprisingly, Molly continued, 'You see, Sammy, as I've tried to tell you before, there is another, different world from the one we know. Where we live, and around us, all is friendly. Animals tolerate each other. Now, in that other world, things are not the same at all. There's rivalry and hunting and killings. And Quartermile Field is like a boundary between the two. So if you stay this side of the boundary you need never know anything about the sort of savagery that goes on there. And now I've told you, you must forget your curiosity. Be content. You have a happy life.'

'Thank you, Molly,' said Sammy. He thought he understood. And he *did* try to put it out of his mind. The trouble was, the thought kept recurring to him that his father must be part of this other dangerous world. And so, if he still meant to find him one day, he would have to face it himself.

It was quite some time later when Sammy suddenly remembered Tiptoe. Why had he not come into the shed? Had he forgotten their arrangement? Or perhaps he had not had an adventure worth telling. Sammy felt he had a lot to tell Tiptoe, anyway. And there was another thing. Perhaps the mouse, being a wild creature, could throw some light on the mystery of Quartermile Field. Sammy was so eager to see him that he started to comb the garden for him, beginning with the clump of alyssum by the cottage. Of course, Tiptoe was not there.

Sammy soon found he had set himself an impossible task. The mouse was so tiny there were a thousand secret places in which he might hide himself. He might have ventured into the mistress's cottage. He could be anywhere. The young tabby decided he must wait until nightfall and hope that Tiptoe would this time come into the shed. But, as it turned out, he did not have to wait that long.

Sammy was snoozing contentedly under the apple tree when he felt his tail tweaked. He opened his eyes slowly, suspecting Josephine. His sister, though, was nowhere to be seen. Instead he saw Tiptoe sitting on the tip of his tail, as bold as brass. But when Sammy looked at him, the mouse seemed ready to run off.

'Don't go,' said the cat quickly. 'I want to talk to you.'

'I saw you ranging the garden earlier on,' squeaked the mouse. 'You weren't *hunting* me, were you?'

Sammy looked puzzled. 'Hunting? Of course not. What do you mean?'

'Oh, never mind.' Tiptoe relaxed. He looked very relieved. 'We mice have to be so careful, you know. And you looked very determined.'

Sammy was pleased with this description. 'You've got it all wrong,' he said. 'I was determined to *find* you, that's all. Why didn't you come last night?'

'Oh, it didn't seem – er – safe,' Tiptoe answered diffidently.

'Well, anyway, do you want to hear about my adventure?' Sammy continued. 'I've been quite a long way away and I saw a goat and – and a fierce dog.' He went on to describe in detail what had happened the previous day.

Tiptoe did not seem very comfortable in the open. While Sammy was talking he was up and down on his hind legs, sniffing the air in all directions and looking round to see what was happening in the garden. He just could not keep still.

'I don't believe you've listened to a single word,' Sammy accused him.

'Oh yes, I have,' said the mouse. 'You were chased by a terrier. I know the dog you mean. About your size and as tame as anything. It makes a lot of noise and that's all. If you'd faced up to it, it would have run away.'

'All right,' said Sammy crossly. 'And what wonderful escapade have you had, then?'

'Quickly – follow me,' Tiptoe bade him. He could see Stella pacing slowly over the lawn. He darted away down to the end of the garden and disappeared into a tiny gap under the shed which Sammy had never noticed. When the young cat reached the shed all he could see were Tiptoe's whiskers protruding from the hole.

'That's much better,' said the mouse. 'Now my adventure was much closer to home – in fact in your mistress's cottage. A number of us have nests under the floors and behind the walls. Yesterday I heard there were more scraps to be had for the taking there than ever before. It was as if your mistress had spread them around for us deliberately. I was collecting some to take to a safe corner to enjoy, when in she came. My only escape route was to run up a broom handle. I sat on the top, quivering all over. I didn't know where to go next. Then – guess what? Your mistress stretched out a hand and grasped the broom!'

'You're making this up,' Sammy said disbelievingly.

'I'm not! I'm not!' squeaked Tiptoe. 'If you think that, I won't go on.'

But Sammy was fascinated despite himself. 'Oh, please do,' he begged. 'I'm sorry.'

'Well, there was one thing for me to try then,' the mouse resumed. 'I couldn't run down the broom again. So, as soon as the old lady took hold of it, I ran up her arm to her shoulder and then down her back, jumped to the floor and skipped out of sight. What do you think of that?'

'It's a remarkable story,' Sammy said wryly, 'and I think you invented it.'

'There you go again. I *didn't* invent it,' shrilled Tiptoe angrily.

'The last part you did, *I* know.'

'Oh, very well. Perhaps I elaborated on it a bit. But the essence of it is perfectly true.'

Sammy had lost interest. 'I don't know what to believe

now,' he said grumpily. 'What's the point of telling fibs?'

Tiptoe did not have an answer to that.

'Look,' said Sammy. 'I want to ask you something. Do you know anything about Quartermile Field?'

There was a stony silence.

'Tiptoe? Are you still there?'

'Of course I'm still here. And what do you want to mention that place for? Do you intend going there?' His voice sounded quite different. Gone was the usual chirpy tone. Now there was a new note of sullenness; almost unfriendliness.

'No, I don't want to go there. I just—'

'Good,' interrupted Tiptoe, more brightly. 'Because if you did, we couldn't be friends any more. And for now, I think I'd better leave you.'

Sammy was left to ponder afresh on the strange influence the fateful name seemed to exert over his friends. Why did none of them wish to talk about it? If only someone would explain to him fully, he could put it to the back of his mind. But, so long as the air of mystery prevailed, he could not rest.

To whom could he turn now? There was no one. Ah, if only his father were around. He was the creature who could tell all.

Searching

Time passed. Sammy wandered into the neighbouring gardens and met other pets. None of them wished to discuss the forbidden topic. Sammy even tried to ask the yappy terrier, but it did not want to talk at all once it realized the young cat had seen through its pretence of fierceness. Sammy had grown into a fine male tabby. Now that he was almost full grown, his face looked more crossed out than ever – the colouring had deepened, making the stripe appear bolder.

Josephine went further afield these days and Sammy took her with him into Belinda's paddock – Stella had seemed uninterested in the invitation. While the young cats were running through the long grass, almost under the nose of the goat, a strange noise arrested them. It was a harsh sort of howl which the two cats had never heard before. The noise was repeated. It was evidently a kind of call, but neither Sammy nor his sister could make out the meaning of it.

They sat bolt upright, their silky ears turned sharply towards the sound. Belinda looked up briefly and then resumed her grazing. She had heard the noise before and was not alarmed. It seemed to be coming from beneath the thorn hedge on the perimeter of the field. Sammy and Josephine stared and stared but could distinguish nothing. Then, through the thickly clustered leaves along the bottom of the hedgerow, they detected some movement. A dark shape was pushing its way through the greenery, yet never quite came into view.

Sammy wanted to investigate but his fear held him rigid. Josephine had arched her back and was actually starting to recoil. Then they saw an extraordinary thing. From a different quarter of the meadow Stella emerged and began, calmly and steadily, to walk towards the hedge. Meanwhile the howls continued.

Sammy longed to ask Belinda what it all meant, but he could not find his voice. The significance of the scene was lost upon him, yet he knew it was of importance. Stella reached the field's perimeter and scrambled into the hedgerow. The howling stopped. No harm seemed to come to her.

'Why did she go?' Josephine whispered to her brother.

'I – I don't know,' he muttered. 'I think she must have been called.'

'I don't like it here,' said Josephine, thinking of the easy familiarity of their garden. 'Let's go back.'

'You go,' Sammy replied. 'I want to see what happens.'

But nothing did happen. Josephine departed and Sammy sat on, staring at the spot in the hedge through which his mother had disappeared. At last he plucked up the courage to go and investigate. When he got there, there was nothing to be seen, but a gap in the hedge bottom which Stella must have crawled through. Sammy could detect his mother's scent. And there was another sharper, more acrid scent which was new to him. Should he follow? He was not at all sure what he ought to do. Would Stella be angry if he tried to trail her? He thought there could be no reason for that. He decided to have a look at whatever lay on the other side. With a distinct caution, he edged his way slowly through the thorny growth. He sat down and looked all about him. There was not a trace of Stella, nor any other creature.

On Sammy's left was the road and, across it, the waste ground. But here he was on the edge of another field. It was exactly like the meadow where he had been with Josephine, only larger. As far as he could tell, there was nothing in it – anywhere. Then, suddenly, an enormous black animal reared up in the middle of it. It had long legs, an arched neck and a huge head. It gave a high-pitched whinny, flicked its thick plume of a tail several times and then began to run across the field. Sammy turned and raced back to Belinda's meadow, his heart thumping frantically. Had he strayed into Quartermile Field? Was that terrifying beast the cause of his mother's warning? In his distress, he almost collided with Belinda.

'What's the matter?' she asked him kindly. 'You look panic-stricken.'

'I – I've seen a monster!' cried Sammy. 'He drove me off.' His imagination had got the better of him.

'A monster? Nonsense!' the goat retorted. 'There are no monsters around here.'

'Yes, yes,' the cat insisted, 'in the next field!'

'Oh – oh,' Belinda chortled. 'I see what's happened. You've made the acquaintance of my neighbour. Don't worry about Saul. He's quite harmless. Have you never seen a horse before?'

'A – horse? I . . . no,' Sammy stuttered. Of course, he had heard about such animals. Now he felt foolish and Belinda could see it.

'It's all right, Sammy. You weren't to know, were you? He belongs to the farmer. Now don't fret yourself any more. Saul wouldn't dream of hurting you.'

'So that's not Quartermile Field?'

Belinda looked at him strangely. 'What – Saul's paddock? No. It isn't. And who's been telling you about that?'

Sammy explained. It was only then that he recalled his original reason for going into the field. Where had his mother gone? He soon found that Belinda knew a thing or two.

'You may still be too young to know much about a male animal's call to the female. But that's what you heard. And I shouldn't be at all surprised if it wasn't your father back on his rounds again.'

Beau! So that was why his mother. . . .

'Oh! If only I had known,' wailed Sammy.

'Known? Why, what difference would that have made?' asked Belinda.

'I could have seen my father at last.'

The goat tossed her head. 'I think perhaps it was as well you didn't just then,' she replied mysteriously.

Sammy did not entirely understand. But Belinda went on: 'You will learn in time about such things; that there are times when youngsters should keep to themselves. So it was for the best.'

However, now that Sammy believed his father was in the neighbourhood, he was restless. He left the meadow and returned home, wondering if Stella had come back. Josephine soon told him there had been no sign of her. Sammy explained about the howls.

Josephine looked at him in dismay. 'Will she come back now?' she asked.

'I hope they both come,' said Sammy fervently.

'*I* don't,' Josephine returned. 'What do we want Beau here for? He'll only upset everything.' She did not want any interference in her carefree life.

Sammy said nothing. He knew that he and his sister held different opinions about their father.

The day wore on and Stella did not appear. Molly had heard the caterwauling and had realized it must be Beau. She wondered if she should offer some comfort to the two young cats, or whether it would be better to leave them to their own devices. After all, they were no longer tiny kittens and had to know how to fend for themselves. So Molly kept to herself.

In the evening Mrs Lambert provided four saucers of food as usual. When Stella did not put in an appearance she called for a while. Eventually she removed the untouched saucer in case Sammy or Josephine tried to be greedy.

Later the two cats settled themselves in the shed for the night. It was strange without their mother and Josephine was a little frightened. Sammy was not at all sympathetic and scoffed at her.

'Don't be kittenish,' he taunted her. 'You're nearly full grown. Supposing Stella never comes back? You'll have to get used to it.'

'Don't say that,' Josephine pleaded. 'I miss her.'

That night Sammy dreamt of his father. Josephine stayed awake for a long time, listening for Stella. At last she, too, slept.

Towards dawn the unmistakable sound of Stella's call woke them both. Josephine rushed to meet her mother. But Stella seemed to have changed. She did not exactly rebuff her daughter, yet her manner was very aloof. It was as if she had other things on her mind.

Sammy gambolled around her, crying, 'Where's Beau? Where's Beau?'

Stella did not answer for a while. At last she said reluctantly, 'He's around.'

'Around where? Can I see him?'

'I suppose there's nothing to stop you,' said Stella in an offhand way. 'But he's probably hunting now.'

Hunting! A thrill of excitement went through Sammy. That unknown world. Hunting! If only he could find his father and join in, *that* would be something to tell Tiptoe about.

'Would Beau allow me to hunt with him?' he asked his mother. He was on tenterhooks.

Now Stella got cross. 'Don't be ridiculous, Sammy,' she said. 'What do you need to hunt for? You're fed well every day. This is not some sort of game for your father. It's a deadly serious business. He must hunt to survive, and if he fails he starves.'

The blunt words dashed Sammy's hopes. But he was thoughtful enough to say, 'I hope he never starves. He could have some of my food, rather than that.'

Stella was mollified by his unselfishness. 'You're a generous-hearted cat,' she acknowledged, 'and I think you really do care about your father's welfare. He should be pleased to have a son with a genuine regard for him.'

Josephine felt chastened. She had never shown the slightest interest in Beau. Indeed she would not have welcomed him if he had walked into the shed that moment. But she could see that Stella was impressed with Sammy's behaviour and she was jealous.

'Why doesn't he go and look for his precious father then,' she muttered, 'and leave us in peace?'

Stella saw how the land lay but was wise enough to make no comment. She only said, 'He steers clear of gardens, Sammy. So it's no good looking for him here.'

Sammy could hardly believe his ears. His mother had as good as directed him. He waited no longer, but went quietly out of the shed into the shadowy garden.

He made straight for Belinda's meadow. He saw her ghostly shape in the blackness of the field and went directly to her.

'Is Beau about? My mother says he's hunting.'

'Is he now? And what are you doing here at this hour?'

'I'm going to join him,' Sammy boasted.

'Don't show your foolishness, Sammy. If Beau is hunting, he'll be away from these parts over towards Quartermile Field. And you won't be going there, I think?'

Sammy looked crestfallen. 'Oh, I – I didn't realize,' he murmured. But he was beginning to get the gist of things. Stella had known this and allowed him to be responsible for his own actions. He felt very grown up.

'I'll wait around for a while,' he told Belinda. 'Perhaps my father will come back after he—' his voice tailed off.

'Do as you like,' said Belinda. She stepped daintily away. Presently Sammy saw her lie down in the lush grass.

Sammy was alone and a little scared. The vastness of the open field and the wide arc of sky made him feel as if he had been somehow swallowed up. But after a bit he began to enjoy it. He had never been so free and independent. He thought, with juvenile scorn, of Josephine's clinging dependence on Stella. This night, Sammy was sure, marked a change in his personality. He believed he had come of age.

When the sky began to lighten, his new confidence urged him on. He went determinedly towards the hedge where Stella had kept her tryst with Beau, and then into the horse's paddock. Sammy was relieved to see that Saul appeared to be sleeping. His great black shape leant motionless against a solitary sycamore. Sammy began to reconnoitre the hedgerow.

Under the thick greenery it was still very dark. Sammy's pupils dilated hugely as he paced cautiously along, but he could see very little. Suddenly a sharp hiss of warning made him jump. A strange cat was spitting at him. Sammy's immediate fright soon gave way to excitement when he realized what this could mean.

'Now then – where are you going?' came a harsh voice.

'I – I – I—' spluttered Sammy, torn between two different emotions.

'I – I – I,' mocked the voice. The animal had soon made out it was dealing with a youngster. 'I – I – I – what?'

'I'm sort of – searching,' Sammy explained in a small voice.

'Searching, are you? What for? Food?'

'No, not food. For my father.'

'For your father, eh? What's your name?'

'Sammy.'

'Never heard of you. Come closer. Let's have a look at you.'

Sammy edged slowly forward. The other cat was curled up under a bush.

'Oh, quite an ugly creature, I see,' it said next. 'Not that I'm one to talk.'

Sammy peered into the gloom. His heart sank. He was looking, not at a tabby, but at a black cat – a very mangy, tattered black cat.

'I'm known as Scruff,' said the animal. 'No need to guess why, eh? Now what's this fuss about your father? Cats aren't usually very interested in who sired them.'

'Aren't they?' Sammy asked innocently. 'I suppose I must be different. I feel a need for male company.'

'Oh, there's plenty of that to be had,' chuckled the black cat. 'What sort of company do you keep, then?'

'All female,' Sammy answered, 'every one of them.'

'All female?' repeated the scruffy animal. 'I'm surprised you grumble about it.' His voice had a leer in it which was completely lost on Sammy.

'There are my mother and sister and Molly the dog,'

Sammy explained naïvely. 'We all belong to the same mistress.'

'Guessed as much by the look of you,' Scruff said, scornfully. 'You're someone's little pet, with your smooth coat and sleek looks. And what, may I ask, happened to the father of this little family?'

'Nothing. He was never part of it. He came – er – from outside.'

'Oh, I get it,' said the cat. 'One of us. What's his name?' he asked suspiciously.

'Beau.'

'Beau? I don't know him, then, and I know a few, I can tell you.'

'Do you? Where is your home?'

'Home?' Scruff seemed to find this very amusing and it was a while before he recovered himself. Then he said: 'My *home* is nowhere in particular, but I spend most of my time back there – in the waste ground.'

'Oh yes, I know,' Sammy said eagerly. 'I can see into that place from the apple tree. I've seen movement there. It might have been you.'

'Might have been. Might not. There's plenty of us around.' A sly look stole over his face. He got up and stretched. 'Perhaps you'd like to meet some of them?' He saw there could be a bit of sport ahead with this naïve young animal.

'Yes, I would,' said Sammy. He was thinking that there might be another animal there who knew of his father. 'But what about the road? I – I'm not used to—'

'Oh, don't worry about that,' the black cat reassured him at once. 'It'll be as empty as this field at this time of day. Come on. Follow me.'

—7—

The Vagabonds

The black cat walked with a limp. He was a poor-looking beast: thin, dirty, with bald patches on his flanks. Sammy was bigger, stouter by far and had still not attained his full size. They crossed the road together, entering the bomb site through weeds and rubble. The daylight had hardened now and Sammy saw everything clearly.

'This is a good hunting ground,' Scruff told him. 'Lots of cover, see? Little creatures need cover but when they leave it – bang! That's when we pounce.'

Sammy was most impressed with this. Of course he knew nothing about hunting, but he had an idea he was going to find out. A tingle of excitement ran through his veins. He looked about keenly.

The waste ground was overgrown with a tangle of weeds and brambles. Elder-bushes, birch and sycamore saplings had colonized this plot amongst the relics of buildings, and birds flitted to and fro through the branches. Occasionally one would alight briefly on the ground and peck up an insect or seed, but would soon be off again. The ground around here, each bird knew, was rife with danger.

Sammy heard a slight rustle from a clump of growth close to his shoulder. He tensed. Then he became aware of the distinct scent of another cat. A very small white cat emerged. It stopped to sniff the air, closing its eyes against the strengthening sunlight. It turned slowly and looked at Sammy. Their eyes met and held each other's gaze unblinkingly. The white cat's eyes were blue, the ears and nose pink beneath the white hair.

'This is Pinkie,' Scruff said. 'Pretty, isn't she? But already claimed. And no contest. She's the leader's.'

Sammy had not a clue what all this meant.

'What's wrong with your face?' Pinkie asked him cheekily.

'My face? Oh, the stripe. I'm stuck with it, I'm afraid,' said Sammy. He was quite used to such remarks.

'The rest of you's all right.' Pinkie was looking him up and down coolly. 'Did you bring him here, Scruff?'

'Sort of,' was the gruff answer. 'He's got a home but he wants to see how *we* live.'

Something in the way he said this passed a message to the white cat.

'We can show him a lot,' she purred.

Their voices had brought others out of hiding, or roused them from sleep. A group began to assemble. There were tabbies, a ginger, a tortoiseshell and white and an old white cat with a prominent splash of black across his back. Sammy looked at each of them warily. He felt vulnerable. By comparison with Stella, Josephine and the cats he had seen before, these animals looked hard and mean. It was clear they led lives of toughness, even suffering. They were smaller than Sammy, bony and scarred; but the most noticeable thing about them was their eyes. In every animal's eyes there was the same lacklustre gleam: the gleam of hunger. And they stared at Sammy, it seemed, with resentment. He became uneasy. His back fur prickled. He shifted his stance.

'You're – you're all hunters, I expect?' he enquired awkwardly. The cats ringed him round.

'Of course we're hunters,' said Scruff.

'And vagabonds,' said the white cat with the black marking.

'It – er – it must be very exciting,' Sammy remarked. He was aware that he sounded foolish. His inexperience amongst these veterans of hard living made him feel like a tiny kitten again. He seemed to shrink.

'Exciting?' exclaimed one of the tabbies, a female. 'Are you excited, Brindle?' She spoke to another tabby.

'Oh yes, very,' he growled. 'I'm excited right now. There's nothing like starving from time to time to make you excited, is there, Brownie?'

The female tabby looked into the distance as if pondering the question. 'I don't know,' she said slowly. 'Getting soaked to the marrow in a rainstorm in winter can be very exciting.'

'Doesn't compare with being target practice for stone-throwing humans,' Scruff remarked in a tone that implied he actually enjoyed it. 'That really is the *height* of excitement,' He turned to Sammy. 'Look, I'll show you.' He extended his damaged leg for scrutiny. Then he walked right round the visitor with a very accentuated limp.

Sammy's face fell. 'I must seem stupid,' he muttered. 'My life's so easy. Trouble-free, uneventful, but – deadly dull.'

'How awful for you,' said Pinkie with mock sympathy. The innocent Sammy was completely taken in.

'It's not that bad. Just boring,' he said. 'How I'd enjoy some of your experiences!'

The cats exchanged glances. This pet cat was ingratiating himself. But there seemed to be an opportunity for some light relief for *them* here. They believed they had an idiot amongst them.

'You see, my father's like you,' Sammy went on. 'You know – a – a vagabond. I think some of his qualities have rubbed off on me. Perhaps some of you know of him? He's called Beau.'

None of the animals appeared to know anything about a cat called Beau. Only in Pinkie's eyes was there a brief flicker, maybe of recognition, at the sound of the name. But Sammy failed to notice and Pinkie said nothing.

'You've told us your father's name,' said the ginger cat. 'What's yours?'

'Sammy.'

'I'm called Sunny,' said the ginger cat. 'You can probably see why.'

'Your colour?'

'Clever, aren't you?' was the sarcastic reply. 'Same with her.' He indicated the tortoiseshell and white. 'Easiest name for her was Mottle, so that's what we call her.'

'So you'll understand why I'm called Patch,' said the white cat with the black marking. 'Well now, you'd like to try our way of life, would you?' He opened his mouth in a sort of grin, revealing that he had lost a good few of his teeth. It was obvious that he was quite old. 'And maybe you will. Perhaps we could all get some amusement out of it.' He looked round at the others meaningfully. 'Of course, there are conditions attached,' he went on. 'You'd have to prove– er– your suitability, sort of thing. I think that's fair, don't you?'

'More than fair,' Sammy answered promptly. He could hardly suppress his excitement. 'You're the leader of the – er – vagabonds, I take it?'

The other cats were highly amused at this. Sunny rolled over on to his back and twisted around in his delight. Patch glared at him, pretending to be angry. 'All right, don't forget I *was* the leader once,' he reminded them all. He sauntered over to Sammy and sat down right by him. 'No, I'm no longer leader,' he informed him. 'Too old now. And not strong enough. You'll see

Brute some time though. He's not around at present.'

'Brute?' repeated Sammy.

'Yes – a good name too,' said Patch. 'Doesn't do to cross him. But we all know our place, you see, so there aren't too many ructions. Brute's the King Cat all right. He gets all the best pickings.'

'The pickings?' Sammy did not understand.

'Pick of the grub, pick of the basking spots, pick of the shelter, pick of the female company.'

'I see.' Sammy remembered what Scruff had said about Pinkie. She seemed to be in a place of honour.

'Now then, about your qualifications,' Patch resumed.

'Yes?'

'Can you fight?'

'Er – I don't know, I've never—' began Sammy.

'No problem. We'll soon find that out. Can you hunt?'

'I – I've never had to,' Sammy faltered.

'"Course you haven't. You're a pet, aren't you?' said Patch. 'The thing is, if you had to – could you?'

'I'm sure I could learn.'

'That's the way. Now, let's see. Can you swim?'

'I – I—' Sammy stuttered.

'I've never had to!' all the other cats chorused at once. They were laughing at him. Sammy felt small.

'You see, Sammy, you might have to do a bit of fishing. So it's best to know how.' Patch seemed to be quite genial.

'Swimming comes naturally, doesn't it?' Sammy queried.

'Natural as can be. Now – can you climb?'

'Oh yes!' Sammy cried, pleased to lay claim to one skill.

'Thought so,' said Patch shortly. 'You'll have to prove it, mind.'

'That's easy,' said Sammy. 'Any time.'

'Don't be too sure,' Brindle cautioned him. 'We mean real climbing. Not trees or fences.'

Sammy was puzzled. What else was there? But Patch was speaking again.

'You'll have to cease to be a pet. You can't live in two places,' he said. His mind was working on an idea to the vagabond cats' real advantage.

'I understand that,' said Sammy. But when he thought of Stella and Josephine and Molly his heart gave a little tug.

'You have a master?' Patch asked.

'No. A mistress. She's very kind.'

'Does she feed you properly?'

'No need to ask him that, Patch,' Brownie interjected. 'Just look at his full coat.'

'Yes, and how plump he is,' remarked Brindle. 'I can almost smell the good things he gets to eat from here.'

'What do you eat, Sammy?' Pinkie wanted to know.

'All sorts,' he answered. 'Meat and liver and fish. You know, the usual things we all eat.'

'The – usual things?' Scruff muttered. He was drooling. He had never known the taste of rich food. The other cats were all swallowing hard too.

'Look,' said Patch, with difficulty. His mouth was running with water. 'Here's what I think you should do.' He swallowed. 'You should stop eating such food straight away.' Swallow. 'If you really mean to live like us . . .' Swallow. '. . . show us that your old attachment is over.' Swallow. 'And – and—'

'Bring some of the food to us!' cried Sunny.

'Er – yes, that's right,' Patch agreed hastily. 'You know, to sort of demonstrate your sincerity.'

'Then we'll know you mean business,' explained Sunny.

'All right,' said Sammy. 'When shall I do it?'

'Sooner the better, I should think,' said Scruff with feigned nonchalance. His jaws ached with longing. 'Wouldn't you, Patch?'

'Certainly. When are you fed?'

The vagabond cats milled around in their eagerness. Their stomachs were in knots of anticipation. Sammy felt a dozen eyes fastened on him.

'I could go back now and beg for a titbit,' he suggested.

'No titbits,' said Brindle. 'Something more solid, we're thinking of.'

'The main meal is in the evening,' Sammy informed them.

Their faces fell. But Patch said, 'Very well. Come to us tonight. We shall all be waiting.'

The cats began to disperse. Scruff limped away too. Pinkie, however, remained behind.

'You might as well see a bit more while you're here,' she offered.

'Thanks,' said Sammy. 'It could be useful.'

The little white cat led him off across the uneven ground, skirting the main clumps of vegetation. She had a dainty, light sort of walk which rather fascinated her companion. He stole several sidelong looks at her as they went along. Eventually he said, 'You look in better shape than the others.'

'Do I? You've been studying me then?' she asked, archly.

'Well, it's quite noticeable,' Sammy answered. 'You don't look so much like a vagabond.'

'That'll be Brute's doing then,' said Pinkie. 'He gets the best food so I sometimes get a share.'

On the other side of the waste ground was a very high wire mesh fence which was broken in many places. Behind this the remnants of some old allotments lay.

Growths of cabbage, lettuce and other vegetables, long ago turned wild, still sprouted here amongst the grasses, nettle and dock. Pinkie stopped by one of the broken sections of fence.

'This is where you go through,' she informed Sammy. 'Rabbits come here most evenings to feed. The young ones are no match for the likes of us. Now I'll show you something else.'

They went along a depression in the ground towards a dilapidated wooden building which leant at a crazy angle away from the lie of the land. It was not unlike Sammy's shed at home. But there was no door on this old ruin, very little left of the roof and no floor. Pinkie looked at Sammy significantly.

'This is my place of shelter,' she announced with a fine sense of ownership. 'Actually I was born here – underneath, d'you see? I had brothers and sisters but now I'm the only survivor. My mother got run over.'

'Does Brute—' Sammy began.

'Yes.' Pinkie forestalled him. 'It's his shelter too – when he's around. He comes and goes. He has other females to visit. But I'm his favourite.'

Sammy asked, 'And the others? Do they use this shelter?'

'The other vagabonds? No. They daren't. It's the King Cat's.'

Sammy understood.

Pinkie returned to the subject of food. 'Sometimes we find scraps. . . .'

Sammy had already noticed a group of houses which bordered the plot near Pinkie's shelter. Apart from these the waste ground was surrounded by fields and patches of woodland. The two cats continued the circuit of the site. Presently Pinkie stopped again and sat down.

'On that bank over there,' she said, 'you can often see

mice of different sorts. They come out of little holes and there's a perfect place to lie in wait for them – here, behind this tree stump. But you've got to be alert. They're very, very quick.'

Sammy thought of Scruff and his limp. He wondered how he made out.

'Who's the quickest of you?' he asked his guide.

'Brute, of course,. He's best at everything. That's why he's the King Cat.'

'What about Scruff?'

'He's the least agile of us,' Pinkie answered. 'He doesn't do very well. He usually feeds off remains, if there are any to be had.'

Sammy was sympathetic. He thought he would try and help him when he brought the food. He would look for Scruff first.

Pinkie took Sammy back to the point where he had first entered the bomb site. He was eager to get home now. He remembered the road had to be re-crossed and he wanted to be gone before the traffic posed much of a threat. Already he could hear the sounds of cars passing by at frequent intervals. But he hesitated, wondering whether to ask Pinkie for guidance. Now it was her turn to examine him. Secretly she was pleased with Sammy's appearance and, while he paused, she looked him over closely. Finally Sammy decided not to ask for help. He recalled he was expected to prove himself. He turned to go.

'I shall see you later, I suppose?' he murmured.

'Yes, you can count on it,' Pinkie replied.

As he went, Sammy looked round once. The little white cat was sitting in the same spot, watching him, and blinking in the bright sunlight.

—8—

Brute

Sammy got across the road safely and was soon back in his own garden. He had decided not to say anything to Stella about the plan for the evening. He knew perfectly well she would not want him to mix with the vagabonds—she had already warned him about his father's style of life. He spent the day dodging showers of rain and avoiding Josephine's questions. Stella made no enquiries at all; her interest in her offspring was quite evidently on the wane. Sammy was longing for a sight of Tiptoe. He had so much to tell him. But, as luck would have it, the mouse did not show up.

The evening arrived. Mrs Lambert was preparing the animals' food in the kitchen. Sammy heard the familiar sound of chopping and the chink of food plates, and then the mistress called her pets to their meal. It was raining again and they were to eat indoors. Stella and Josephine made short work of their meat and sat, licking their chops, while Sammy fussed about his, trying to decide which pieces to leave. He wished his mother and sister would go away. He did not want their suspicions aroused. But, because of the weather, they were in no hurry to leave.

Molly always took longest over her meal. She was slow at everything and eating was no exception. Her portion of meat was, of course, the largest and the chunks were bigger than those given the cats. Out of the corner of one eye Sammy was watching the old dog's progress. He knew that he could not carry much meat at one time to his new friends; only as much as his jaws could hold. It would be difficult to pick up many of his own small pieces and make the journey with them – but a few of Molly's would be much more worthwhile. If only Stella and Josephine would disappear, he might be able to divert the dog and make a quick raid on her plate.

'You don't seem very hungry, Sammy,' his mother suddenly remarked. He froze as if caught in a guilty act.

'Just taking my time, that's all,' he answered unconvincingly. 'No need to wait for me.'

'We're not waiting – don't flatter yourself,' Josephine answered sharply. 'It's wet outside.' She guessed her brother was up to something and was annoyed that she had been unable to discover what it was.

'What about the shed?' Sammy tried.

'It's more comfortable in here,' Stella answered this time.

Now Mrs Lambert noticed that Sammy seemed to be off his food. She watched him with concern. Meanwhile Molly chewed slowly and placidly. Sammy could see that he would have to make his move in front of them all.

There was a particularly large, succulent-looking chunk of meat in Molly's dish which she seemed in no hurry to take. Sammy had his eyes on that piece. He continued to eat his own meal in a half-hearted way, trying to decide whether he could snatch the chunk before Molly got to it, and then make his escape through the door. And if so, could he carry it all the way to the waste ground? Well, he would have to try. A moment came when Molly turned her head away as she chewed. Sammy ran to her bowl, snatched up the selected piece of meat, dropped it, got a better grip on it and dashed out into the rain.

Mrs Lambert was so astonished at this behaviour that it was a while before Sammy heard her voice, calling him back. It was not without misgiving that he continued on his way, up and over the fence and into the next garden where the chickens were already roosting. He knew he had done wrong and he would have preferred to have stolen from any other creature but Molly. But he had got to prove to the vagabond cats that he was true to his word, and he hoped to be able to explain everything to Molly eventually.

Sammy was not aware that two small beady eyes watched his exit from the garden – Tiptoe saw his departure. Sammy could not have spoken to the mouse anyway: the lump of meat was in his mouth, dangling from his jaws and knocking against his chest as he ran. He reached the road very quickly. Already his coat was soaked. He paused timidly at the roadside, listening for those frightening roars of the machines which scared him out of his wits, but all appeared quiet. Sammy raced across, entered the bomb site and threaded his way through the saturated clumps of weed. He stopped, opened his mouth and let the meat fall to the wet ground.

There was a different feel about the place in the gathering darkness. Sammy sensed that something had changed since his previous visit early in the day. He waited. He had forgotten about looking for Scruff and felt uneasy. None of the cats showed up. Then at last he heard a noise – just discernible above the steady patter of rain. Sammy looked around, nervously. A plant rustled, as if lightly brushed by something moving past.

A large, powerful-looking cat, one he had not seen previously, was coming straight towards him. The animal looked mean and hard. Its eyes glittered as it stared at the intruder, its gaze never wavering as it approached. Sammy almost fled, but something in the cat's look kept him rooted to the spot. It was a tabby cat, but its markings were darker, blacker than Sammy's. One of its ears was split and the tip missing, and there were other scars on its face and chest that testified to many a fight. Part of the cat's tail was without fur. Yet, despite its marred appearance, the animal had a majestic calm about it, derived from an awareness of its supremacy and authority. Sammy knew beyond any doubt that he was facing Brute.

The cat sat down in front of him in an unhurried, almost nonchalant manner. Sammy thought he had never seen such a marvellous creature.

In a deep, throaty growl the cat spoke to him. 'Who are you and what are you doing here?'

Sammy gulped. His reason for coming there suddenly seemed to him quite ludicrous. Where were the other cats? He needed their backing. The dark tabby was examining the lump of meat.

'Where did you get this?' it enquired quietly, but there was an air of menace underlying the question. Sammy knew he would have to give a plausible account of himself.

'I brought it here,' he answered unsteadily.

'You brought it here,' repeated the cat. 'For what purpose?'

'For your – er – friends to eat,' Sammy told him, realizing the reply must sound absurd.

'My – friends, you say? What do you know about me?' The tabby's eyes were narrowing.

'I – well, I don't know anything, really,' Sammy gabbled. 'But you *are* Brute, aren't you?'

The cat ignored his question. 'Where do you come from?' it asked, scrutinizing his coat and general appearance of well-being. 'You're no vagabond.'

'I have a home,' Sammy remarked, 'it's true. But I wish to follow another sort of life. The cats here came to an arrangement with me. I was to bring them food to prove my worth and, in return, they would – er – teach me their ways.'

'A remarkable story,' was the response. 'And so you've brought your dinner with you as a token of your desire to adopt our ways?'

Put like that it does sound ridiculous,' Sammy said hopelessly. 'If only the other cats were here, they could explain—'

'It seems, then, that they must have had little faith in your intention of sticking to this strange agreement.' The dark tabby was mocking him. 'It also seems that you have a very great deal to learn about the way we live if you think that this small piece of meat could be shared out amongst the whole company!'

'No, no, I don't think that,' Sammy assured the cat, feeling that he was looking more stupid by the moment. 'I couldn't carry very much. It's a long way. But I took the largest piece I could manage to – er – show I'm true to my word and—'

'And now,' interrupted the cat, 'you'd better go back, I think, to wherever you came from and get some more, don't you? There are quite a lot of us here and, since I always have first choice, even this piece won't be of any use to those you term "my friends".'

Sammy's heart sank. 'But – but – there won't be any more,' he mumbled.

'Won't be any more?' echoed the tabby. 'And you think this derisory morsel is a sufficient mark of your esteem for the starving creatures you expect to teach you all their skills and cunning?'

Sammy lapsed into silence. He wished he had never returned. These animals were a separate race from those like himself, Stella and Josephine. Why had he thought he could enter their world? Why could not he be content with. . . . His racing thoughts were interrupted by the sudden arrival of Pinkie.

'So you did come back, Sammy?' she said, and Sammy thought – hoped – that he could detect just a suggestion of pleasure at his return.

'Sammy?' muttered the dark tabby. 'Sammy, are you?'

'Yes.'

'This is Brute,' Pinkie informed the young male.

'I know,' said Sammy.

'How do you know? Did I say so?' growled the King Cat.

'I – I – guessed,' Sammy answered.

'He's brought us all an offering,' said Brute to the little white cat. 'But I'm afraid only I shall appreciate its flavour.' And he grabbed the lump of meat, chewed it once or twice and then swallowed it hastily.

At once, as if this were a signal, all Sammy's acquaintances of the morning began to appear. They looked about and murmured to each other, glancing in Sammy's direction in an accusing way. They were disappointed not to find a scrap or two of Sammy's rich fare left for themselves. Sammy felt he had let them down.

'I could try again tomorrow,' he offered.

'What's the good?' returned Mottle sourly. 'You could never bring enough for us all to taste.'

Sammy had no answer to that. But Brute had. He had been doing some thinking.

'This sort of food is no luxury for you, I suppose?' he asked the young cat grudgingly.

'Oh no,' Sammy answered. 'It's my normal diet.'

'Well, how very fortunate for you. And how do you think you would survive here on our starvation rations?'

'I – I'd do the best I could,' said Sammy. 'I'd do as you all do. I'd soon learn. And you haven't starved, have you?'

'It would seem like starvation to you, compared with your feasting,' Brute remarked. 'And, let me tell you, some of us *have* starved. All of us you see here – we're just the remnants.'

'The – remnants?'

'There used to be more of us,' Pinkie explained. 'I told you about my brothers and sisters, and there were others, too.'

Sammy had not the experience to understand. In his life food had been brought whenever he had wanted it. Shelter and warmth, too, were taken for granted. How could he comprehend the hardships, the struggle for survival, that these animals faced every day of their lives? The fasting, the discomfort, the monotonous, exhausting battle with the seasons?

'At least let me try,' he said plaintively. He shook his soaking fur, scattering a spray of raindrops around him. The other cats, by contrast, took no notice of the wet. They accepted it as they had to accept everything else which was beyond their control, with a sort of dumb resignation.

'No, you could never break free,' Brute growled scathingly.

'How do you know if you won't put me to the test?' Sammy remonstrated.

Brute had him where he wanted him. 'Right, Tabby

with the Silky Fur,' he said, using the words in a disparaging way, 'let's see how long it takes you to lose your well-groomed appearance. We'll find out how vain you are. And as for us—' he looked round at the vagabonds '—we'll smarten ourselves up a little. Then we can meet each other halfway.'

'How?'

'How?'

'How will we do that?' cried the cats all at once.

'Easy,' said Brute. 'We swap places.'

A stunned silence ensued. Then the vagabond cats began to talk and cry out excitedly. They saw they were in for some real fun.

Sammy, however, asked with misgiving, 'What do you mean – swap places?' Already he was beginning to feel cold and uncomfortable.

'Can't you guess?' Brute sneered. 'You eat our food. We eat yours.'

The full implication of what he had set in train had not struck Sammy before. Now he shuddered visibly. 'But – but – it's impossible,' he wailed. 'There are too many of you. And what about my mistress? She doesn't know you. Why would she feed you?'

'Because she'll think she's feeding *you*, won't she, simple Sammy?' Brute answered.

'But I'm only one cat,' protested Sammy. 'And you're– you're—'

'Rather more than one,' Scruff said comically.

'We take it in turns,' Brute said with feigned patience, as if talking to an idiot. 'Each day a different cat has your food. You leave it – we eat it. And each day we bring you something in return from *our* larder.'

The cats were highly amused. It was the perfect plan. They could not stop chattering. Sammy could only stare at them. He was speechless. It was quite preposterous. How could all this go on under the noses of Stella, Josephine and Molly, let alone their mistress?

'It won't work,' he muttered at last. 'It can't work.'

'Why not?' Brute growled. For the first time he sounded really angry.

'It – it – just won't,' Sammy mewed. 'There are other pets in my mistress's keeping, and we're fed together. How do I get round that?'

'Up to you,' said Brute. 'You'll have to exercise your ingenuity, if you've got any. And if you haven't, you wouldn't survive here for very long. So it'll be a real test for you, won't it?'

Sammy was horrified. What could he do? He saw Pinkie looking at him. In her eyes was a challenge. Sammy turned away miserably. For the second time he realized he was no match for these creatures. Why had he undertaken this crazy venture? It was too late to back out now. Yet there was no one he could turn to for advice, since the whole business had to be conducted in secrecy. He crept away through the pelting rain. A voice called him back. It was Brute, of course.

'And where do you think you're going?'

'I – home, I suppose.'

'Where's home?'

Sammy explained.

'Oh, so you're from that cosy quarter? The garden with the shed, you say? Simple. Tomorrow evening, then, you keep watch. One of us will be along soon as it's dark. Don't forget!'

How could he forget? Sammy wandered away, oblivious now of the wet. He scarcely paused at the roadside before running across, heedless of danger. He could only think of Stella, Josephine and Molly and what they would say about his stealing the meat. And then, worse still, he had to think of a plan for the next evening. If he did not, there would be trouble of a sort he dared not contemplate. This was the result of his meddling. Now he had started something he could not control. As he went past the chicken run towards his home fence he stopped abruptly. He could hardly bear to re-enter his own garden. Something broke into his thoughts – a sound, slight but insistent. After a while he realized what it was: the squeaking of a mouse. Tiptoe was calling him.

—9—

Exchanges

Tiptoe was inside the chicken coop, picking up scraps of grain. The wire mesh was no barrier to a hungry mouse. The hens were asleep, and so was the cockerel. Tiptoe saw a shadowy figure crossing in front of the enclosure. He recognized Sammy at once.

'Sammy! Look at me. I'm in here.' he called. When the cat failed to respond, Tiptoe squeaked louder. He saw Sammy pause and search round for the sound.

'In *here*, Sammy. Amongst the feathered ones. Tee hee.'

Sammy trotted over and peered through the wire. 'Didn't expect to see *you*,' he murmured distractedly. 'What are you doing there?'

'One of my sources of supply,' Tiptoe answered.

Suddenly Sammy perked up. An idea struck him. Tiptoe could help him. The mouse was no pet; he knew something of that other world of the vagabonds. Perhaps he would have some ideas.

'You look drenched,' Tiptoe remarked to the tabby. 'I'm surprised to see you out in this.'

'There is a reason,' Sammy replied. 'I'll tell you all about it. I need your advice. Have you finished eating?'

'Of course not. I've never finished eating. Tee-hee. But

wait a bit. I'll come out.' Tiptoe pushed his tiny body easily through the wire mesh. 'We can't stand here,' he said. 'What about the shed? Is it safe?'

'Er – no,' Sammy lied. 'No, it isn't. Stella's on the prowl.'

'Over here then,' said Tiptoe, ducking into a flower-pot lying on its side. 'You get under that plant.'

'What's the use?' grumbled Sammy. 'It's as saturated as I am.'

'Please yourself. What do you want to ask me?'

Sammy collected his thoughts. Then he poured out the story of his new acquaintances the vagabonds, of Brute, of the bargain and how he had to prove himself. 'Now I don't know what I'm to do,' he finished up. 'These half-wild cats are going to come into my garden expecting to be fed. But how can they be with my mother and sister around – and Molly? And if they're not fed what will they do? Oh Tiptoe, can you think how I'm to get out of all this?'

The mouse was very still and quiet, something quite foreign to his nature. His mind was racing. He had realized at once the implications for himself and his relatives if the stray cats entered Mrs Lambert's garden. His own comparatively quiet life would be disrupted in the worst possible way. These animals were not friendly pets; they were hunters. And he and his kind were the hunted – they would never know a moment's peace again. He had told Sammy he liked adventure, and did enjoy the sort of mild risks he ran every time he entered Mrs Lambert's cottage. But that was quite different from this. His life would become fraught with the most awful peril. He had to think of a way of helping Sammy that would, at the same time, help himself and the other mice.

'Well, well,' he said, 'you certainly seem to have bitten off more than you can chew, don't you? That's what comes of going into Quartermile Field.'

'What – what do you mean?' Sammy cried. 'I haven't—' He broke off as the whole thing suddenly became clear. Of course, it made sense. His mother's warning. Molly's explanation of it being out of bounds; the other sort of life. He knew now. He *had* been to Quartermile Field. Now he was caught up by its strange force, changed by it, excited by it yet repelled by it too. And he was bringing its influence with him back to his old peaceful, comfortable home.

Tiptoe saw that he understood. 'Too late for regrets,' he said sharply. 'We have to think how to outwit the – er – vagabonds.' He pronounced the word with the utmost distaste.

'There's no time,' Sammy moaned. 'It's to begin tomorrow night.'

'You deserve to go hungry for the trouble you cause,' Tiptoe told him. 'But here's what you must do. You must keep out of sight all day. When your mistress prepares your food you don't show up for it. If I know her ways she'll leave it around for a while in the hope of your coming to claim it. If the food's outside there's no problem, because the strange cat will eat it when it's dark. Your mistress won't know it's not you.' He paused, as a thought struck him: 'But supposing she leaves the food inside?'

'She only does that when it's wet – like tonight,' Sammy answered.

'You'd better wish for dry weather then,' Tiptoe said wryly. 'And, whatever you do, don't show yourself at all.'

'I'll roam about,' said Sammy. 'Perhaps I'll stay in here. But what about the next night and the next. . . . They're coming one by one.'

'Same thing,' Tiptoe replied. 'Keep out of sight. As long as the food disappears, your mistress will go on providing it. Am I right?'

'I hope so,' said Sammy. 'But what of Stella and Josephine? They're going to be suspicious if they never see me.'

'No good worrying about that,' answered the mouse. 'It's only a matter of time before one of them – or the dog – will encounter one of the strangers. They can't be forever asleep.'

'Molly sleeps indoors at night,' Sammy informed him. 'So she'll be out of the way.'

'Well, remember what I said,' Tiptoe admonished the young cat. 'Keep out of the way tomorrow and say nothing to anyone. And now I'd better go and warn all *my* friends.' He ran off through the ceaseless rain, along paths and tunnels known only to the mice. Sammy was left alone to ponder for the first time on the real danger in which, quite unintentionally, he had placed his little friend.

At last, tired of the wet and discomfort, the young tabby scaled the dividing fence and jumped into his own garden. Outside the shed he shook himself. He crept in, hoping to find Stella and Josephine asleep. But they were not.

'Here comes my greedy brother,' came Josephine's voice in the darkness.

'Sammy?' This was Stella's voice now. 'You've become quite a wanderer.' There was no mention of the meal-time incident.

Sammy did not reply. All he wanted was to dry off and go to sleep.

'Why did you do it, Sammy?' his sister continued. 'Our mistress seemed quite upset.'

'Oh, I don't know,' Sammy answered grudgingly. 'I

suppose for a bit of fun, that's all.'

'It wasn't much fun for Molly,' Josephine persisted.

'All right, Josephine. It doesn't matter,' said her mother. 'Molly didn't miss the meat so it's not important.'

Sammy thankfully began to lick himself. What he had done that evening was trivial compared with what was to come.

Early the next morning he left the shed and his mistress's garden behind. He would have liked to have seen Molly and given her an explanation, but it was too early for the old dog to be around and, in any case, he dared not risk it. Mercifully the rain had stopped. The ground and every plant of course, were still soaked, but all was beautiful to look at. The late summer sun was reflected in every dazzling water-drop and the air was fresh and cool and heartening. Sammy ran briskly along. He had decided to spend the day in Belinda's meadow. His flagging spirits were revived by the morning and a refreshing sleep. Tiptoe had found a solution to his dilemma and he – Sammy – had been to Quartermile Field and back. He thought about the waste ground. It was not so terrifying. If what he had encountered was all there was to the place, he really did not know what all the fuss was about.

Belinda was standing in the centre of her lush green field with her head bent to the succulent vegetation. She was enjoying an early morning feed. Despite the recent downpour her coat seemed as clean and silky as ever. She was so absorbed she did not notice Sammy's approach. Eventually she looked up, chewing meditatively.

'Hello,' she said, 'it's the cat who sought his father. And did you find him?'

'I'm afraid not,' Sammy replied. 'But I did find a lot of other cats.'

Belinda put two and two together. 'You've crossed the road?' she asked.

'Yes.'

'Well, I'm surprised you didn't find Beau amongst his cronies,' the goat went on. 'He often is.'

'I don't know who my father's cronies are,' Sammy said, wondering if there could be another group of cats somewhere, 'but they're certainly not the animals I spoke to. None of them knew of him.'

'Strange,' Belinda mused. 'Still, the ways of cats are mostly beyond me. You can be very inscrutable.'

Sammy began to look for a less drenched patch of ground where he could sunbathe. He felt he really needed to stretch out in the sun after the chills and damp of the previous day, and it would be a pleasant way of whiling away the time. He selected a good place where the grass was fairly short, lay down and dozed. From time to time he opened his eyes or changed his position, and sometimes Belinda wandered over to have a word. So the day passed.

In the afternoon Sammy became aware that he was feeling frightfully hungry. There was no light titbit, no dish of milk on offer here. He would simply have to go without. He got up, stretched, yawned, and sauntered to a pool of rainwater for a few laps. He wondered what the vagabond cat would bring for him to eat that night.

At last it was dusk and Sammy knew it was time to make tracks. He thought of Mrs Lambert preparing the animals' meals and he felt so hungry he almost weakened. But he knew he had to carry this difficult arrangement through. He went as far as the garden with the chicken-run and settled down to wait in a secluded corner. Luckily the weather had remained dry.

The cockerel was patrolling his territory as usual. Now and then he cast a glance at the young tabby who was crouching nearby. Suddenly he stopped and screeched out: 'Learnt to fly yet?'

Sammy looked away disdainfully. He was in no mood for such nonsense. But the cockerel evidently thought he had hit upon rather a clever joke. He continued to call periodically in his piercing voice. 'Learnt to fly yet, cat?' And, as if providing himself with the answer he knew would not be forthcoming, he varied this with: 'Cats can't fly! They only climb.' His cries were monotonous and irritating, and in the end, exasperated with the bird's stupidity, Sammy moved to a quieter spot.

The evening grew darker. Sammy tried to picture to himself what was happening in his own garden. Stella, Molly and Josephine would have eaten and probably prepared themselves for sleep. His mother and sister would have washed themselves meticulously as always. Molly, of course, did not bother with this. It was one of the first things Sammy had learnt about the differences between cats and dogs. Dogs did not wash themselves. They seemed to prefer a good scratch.

He thought about the all-important plate of food – his food. It should still be standing close to the kitchen door, waiting to be emptied. But supposing it was not? Supposing his mistress considered it unwise to leave it there? After all, what was to stop Stella or Josephine eating it? No, Stella would not, he knew. She was set in her ways and only ate what she needed. And Josephine? She was not greedy. Sammy comforted himself with the thought. It should be all right. But then there was Molly. No, no, that was even more unlikely, that Molly should eat it. She took an age to eat her own meal.

Sammy tried to relax, yet the temptation to check that the food was there was almost irresistible. He dreaded the outcome if it was not. Suddenly he tensed, hearing a scrabbling noise against the fence nearest to him. It must be the vagabond cat. He looked up. Yes, it was Scruff, perched on the fence top. Sammy was relieved it was not Brute.

'Over here,' Sammy hissed.

Scruff jumped down, awkwardly because of his lameness. He was carrying something in his jaws. He came over and deposited two dead mice at Sammy's feet. Sammy stared at them with misgiving. They looked extremely unappetizing and had a rank smell.

'Here's your rations,' Scruff announced abruptly. 'Now where's mine?'

'I'll show you,' Sammy muttered. 'But is this all there is for me?' He indicated the mice. 'There's not much meat on them.'

'Did the best I could,' Scruff replied gruffly. 'What do you expect? You're lucky to have two of 'em.'

Sammy sighed. Famished as he was, he did not know if he could bring himself to taste them.

'I'll go and see if it's all clear,' he told the black cat.

Scruff's eyes had the intense gleam of hunger in them. He was half-starved. Sammy was sorry for him.

'Be quick,' said Scruff. 'Much as I could do to hold off eating these here on the way.'

Sammy climbed to a vantage point overlooking the back of his mistress's cottage. He was astonished to see a plate and a bowl still standing by the door. The door was closed. There was meat on the plate and milk in the bowl. Oh, how he would relish some milk! And, after all, there was no agreement about providing milk as well. Whilst he hesitated, Scruff's voice sounded impatiently below him.

'Well? What's the delay?'

Sammy had a quick look round to make sure no one

was about. Evidently Mrs Lambert was not keeping
watch for him. His mother and sister, too, were not visible.
Now was the moment.

'Up here,' he called.

Scruff joined him eagerly.

'You can see the food quite plainly. It's all yours,'
Sammy told him. He was hoping Scruff would only
interest himself in the meat. But he was disappointed.
The lame cat descended into Mrs Lambert's garden. He
paused to sniff awhile. Satisfied, he made a beeline for
the bowl of milk, lapped it up without a pause and then
commenced on the solid food.

Sammy was interested in Scruff's eating habits. It was
as if he had not eaten for days. The meat was bolted with
barely a chew, until about a quarter of it remained. This
the cat gathered up carefully and held in his mouth while
he returned to Sammy's side.

'Are you planning a reserve store?' the tabby asked
him.

Scruff had to drop the food to answer. 'This is for
Brute, of course,' he growled.

'Brute?'

'Yes, Brute. Surely you don't think the King Cat will
come to fetch for himself? He doesn't come into these
sorts of places. But what would you know about it?'

Sammy understood. Each of the other cats was obliged
to save a portion of their food to take to their overlord.
Brute had them all running about for him, even the
lame Scruff.

'Eat your mice,' Scruff muttered. Then he collected up
the meat again and ran off.

Sammy sniffed at the vagabond's offering daintily. He
was loth to touch these dead creatures. They were not
even warm. But he knew that there would be no food for
him until the next day if he did not. Mrs Lambert would

soon find the empty plates and assume he had cleared them. She would have no cause to think otherwise. Meanwhile Sammy would have to fast. And then the next night another cat would come. . . .

Sammy gulped and took one of the mice, rather gingerly, in his jaws. His stomach grumbled hungrily. He began to bite at the carcass. There was scarcely any flesh worth speaking of, but what there was, was not quite so bad as he had expected. He devoured the best parts of each animal, but his hunger remained unassuaged. It never occurred to him that he might have eaten two of Tiptoe's comrades.

When he had finished he decided to examine the plate and bowl left by his mistress, just in case Scruff had missed something. But he found both were as clean as if there had never been anything on them in the first place. Ah well, he had kept his bargain. And Tiptoe's plan had worked perfectly. Sammy wondered where the little creature was. Well out of sight in a place of safety, he had no doubt. The young cat next considered his own position. There was nothing in the arrangement to say he could not sleep comfortably. He had his own place of shelter. He could still use it. He might have to eat scraps for a while, but at least he could rest where he chose. He trotted along the lawn to where the familiar bulk of the shed loomed dark against the starlit sky. He was surprised to find himself looking forward to the company of Stella and Josephine.

A Feast for a Morsel

Sammy told his mother and sister as little as possible about his wanderings. Stella was not very interested anyway – in her view Sammy was now a grown male cat and would go his own way. Josephine was more inquisitive but, since Sammy would not give her any information, she soon ceased to question him. In any case she and her brother were fast growing apart.

The next morning, when he was sure Mrs Lambert was not looking for him, he sought out Molly. The old dog was so pleased to see her young friend that Sammy's affection for her increased even further. Molly could not restrain herself from giving the tabby a couple of hearty licks all over his funny, crossed-out face. Sammy knew at once he had no need to apologize for stealing her food.

'I shan't be around so much for a while,' he told Molly enigmatically.

'I understand,' replied the kindly animal. 'It's only to be expected now you're an adult. You've become a big, strong cat. Why should you restrict yourself to this little garden?'

Sammy was surprised at her words, but he knew Molly for a wise old beast.

'I expect you've seen some of the other side of life,

haven't you?' she went on, with a wry expression on her grizzled face.

'You – you know?' gasped Sammy.

'Of course I know. It was only a matter of time before you found out. You're your father's son after all. And I can see you've changed.'

'I *have* changed, Molly,' Sammy admitted. 'I have different ideas now. But I've yet to meet my father.'

'Have you? You surprise me. But you will; you can be sure of it.'

Sammy noticed Mrs Lambert in the kitchen. 'I – er – think I'll stretch my legs,' he said and left Molly abruptly.

She watched him disappear over the fence. His speed, despite his stocky build, was impressive. 'Well, Beau,' the dog murmured to herself, 'you have a son to be proud of there, and maybe, before long, a match for you too.'

By the evening Sammy was so hungry he could scarcely keep still while he waited for the vagabond to bring him his supper. He longed for something other than dead mice but, on the other hand, he did not care what was brought provided it was more substantial than Scruff's offering. He kept away from the chicken run, so that the cockerel should not begin his silly chants again.

He heard his mistress calling his name at meal-time and tapping his plate on the ground to encourage him. The sound was a torment to him but he held himself back. It seemed an age after that before he saw the ginger cat Sunny sitting on the fence top. This cat, in common with most of the other vagabonds, was scornful of Sammy and had not put himself out to catch the young tabby anything worthwhile. When they met he dropped the remains of a sparrow on the ground and watched

Sammy's reaction with amusement. To Sunny it was a great piece of fun to take advantage of this soft, domesticated animal.

'Is that all you could get?' cried Sammy, realizing now that Scruff had been rather generous to him. 'I've had nothing but two dead mice since yesterday.'

'*Two*?' Sunny mocked him. 'Well, you were lucky. This is our usual fare for the day and I know you wanted to find out all about how we live.'

'I don't believe you,' Sammy said angrily. 'That scrap is scarcely a mouthful. It wouldn't keep a kitten alive, let alone a big animal like you.'

'Some days are better than others,' Sunny told him. 'You'll find out if you ever learn how to hunt.' There was an undisguised contempt in his voice. He was second only to Brute in skill and strength and had the confidence to go with it, even though he was just a little smaller than Sammy.

'I'll learn how to hunt,' Sammy answered quickly. 'And I'll do better for myself than this!' He was really seething.

'Do as you like with it,' snapped the ginger cat. 'If you don't want it, I'll eat it myself. I provided it for you – now what have you provided for me?'

'*I* haven't provided anything,' Sammy returned. 'You've got my mistress to thank for your banquet. And I don't consider this scrap of feathers a fair exchange.'

'Don't you now?' purred Sunny. His eyes roved over the tabby, assessing his potential as a fighter. But he could see nothing other than a soft, glossy, well-groomed and well-fed animal who could pose no sort of a threat. 'And what do you think we should do about it?'

Sammy felt cheated and mocked. There were the beginnings of a feeling of hostility inside him which would eventually spur him into action. But not yet. He still had not quite the hardness or the self-confidence necessary. So on this occasion he backed down, saying sullenly, 'There's nothing to be done, is there? I can't control what you catch. You'll find a bowl of food over the next fence by the wall. There are other cats about so you'd better wait until your way's clear.'

'Other cats?' repeated Sunny. 'Well, if they're anything like you they won't be much of a worry.' He stalked off, having delivered this final insult.

Sammy's tail flicked in anger and his fur rose on his back. But Sunny saw none of it. He had made Sammy quail, and the tale he would take back to Quartermile Field was of how the cats could play this game with the pet tabby for all they were worth. He found a plate of fish, ate most of it, then carefully picked up some large pieces to offer as tribute to Brute.

Sammy had eaten the sparrow and, as Sunny returned the way he had come, he saw the young tabby vomiting up the unaccustomed bones and feathers from his pampered stomach. 'Pets!' hissed the ginger between his clenched teeth.

When Sammy had recovered himself he felt very thirsty. He went miserably to look for the nearest puddle. His hollow belly ached. He had never known such hunger. He knew he could not possibly wait another entire day for some measly scrap of food. The question of hunting entered his mind again. It seemed to be the only thing now that stood between him and starvation. But what could he hunt? And where?

All at once he remembered Pinkie's talk of rabbits. A whole rabbit represented a magnificent meal compared with the mere morsels of skin and bone he had been presented with so far. Sammy had seen rabbits in Belinda's meadow – not close by, but near enough to appreciate their size. He knew nothing of their habits or movements but, sooner or later, he would have to find out about them. Why not start now?

He found a pool of clean water and quenched his thirst. Then, with the spirit of adventure inside him, he set off on his quest. He came to the road, watched and listened carefully. It was dark and quiet. He trotted across. He was about to enter the waste ground when a huddled shape in the gutter made him turn his head. Something was lying there. Curious, he sauntered over.

It was the carcass of a rabbit, killed by a car as it tried to cross the road. Sammy smelt the meat. It was fresh. The unfortunate rabbit was a recent victim; so recent that none of the vagabond cats had had time to discover it. Sammy did not delay in capitalizing on his luck. He grasped the body easily with his strong teeth and, with the carcass dangling between his front legs, he re-crossed the road, walking stiffly because of his load. He made straight for Belinda's field and headed for the tallest, thickest growth of herbage where he could be safe from prying eyes.

Never had a meal tasted so good. Nothing given him by Mrs Lambert, however rich or toothsome, could compare with this rabbit. Sammy's great hunger added a tremendous zest to the flavour of the meat and he had the satisfaction of knowing that this meal was the very first he had provided for himself. It put new heart into him and he felt more than ready to meet the next day's challenge. He fell asleep where he was, with the delicious taste of rabbit on his lips.

In the early morning he awoke on a bright clear day to find Belinda standing over him and examining him thoughtfully. She had noticed dried blood around his mouth.

'You have the look of Quartermile Field about you,' she told Sammy.

At first the young cat was puzzled, being only half awake. He stood up and stretched and saw the remains of the rabbit carcass lying where he had slept.

'I have to feed myself,' he answered the goat, almost defensively.

'So I see.' Belinda's attitude had changed. She did not sound friendly any longer.

Sammy thought it was time to go. 'I'll bid you farewell then,' he said awkwardly.

Belinda did not answer but, as the cat moved off, she called him back. 'You can take this with you,' she said, indicating the carcass. 'I'd rather not have your leavings turning sour in my field.'

Sammy took up the half-eaten rabbit and paused, unsure where to take it. Belinda watched him. She could guess what was going through his mind.

'I doubt if Stella or young Josephine would welcome it,' she remarked phlegmatically. 'I'd be surprised if you have much in common with them any more.'

Sammy turned with his burden and made for the hedgerow. He planned to find a hiding-place for it, in case he should need to return to it. He dropped it amongst the prickles of hawthorn and bramble shoots and nudged it out of sight. There was certainly another meal left on the body. He wondered if he would need it that night.

Having deposited his cache of food, Sammy gave himself a thorough wash. When he had finished, he looked once more like a domestic animal. But his thoughts were not on domestic matters. He had decided to wait in a safe place near to the road to see which cat should emerge from the bomb site that evening. He was not going to be so meek and mild from now on. If he was not brought a proper ration this time, then the vagabond responsible would not be allowed to go near his mistress's garden. Sammy was becoming aware of his strength.

He kept out of sight all day in a spot bordering Belinda's meadow. The goat obviously felt no desire for his company any more and he had to accept it. When dusk fell he moved. Against a wall of the last cottage overlooking the road he waited for the vagabond cat to make its appearance.

It was a long time before anything stirred. The night was well on before Sammy at last saw the gleam of green eyes on the opposite side of the road. He saw the eyes first, caught in the glare of headlamps of an approaching car. The car passed and the next thing Sammy knew a dark body came running, quite unwittingly, towards him. Sammy fastened his gaze on the animal's jaws. There was nothing large enough to be noticeable in the darkness. So the cat was either bringing him a minute scrap or – nothing. Now he recognized a tabby body. It was Brindle.

As soon as he saw Sammy, Brindle stopped. The two tabbies faced each other – one plump, strong and shining, the other thin, hard and dull-coloured.

'I've come to meet you,' Sammy said, eyeing the tiny titbit of food Brindle had brought – the head of a small fish. 'I can save you a journey.'

'Save me a journey?' Brindle growled. 'What are you talking about?'

'I'm talking about your intention to rob me of my food,' Sammy replied icily. 'You've a strange idea of fairness, you vagabonds. My day's ration of meat for this – this – insult!'

Brindle's eyes narrowed. It seemed the pet was looking for trouble. Well, that was fine by him. He would soon teach him a thing or two. 'It's an insult, is it?' he whispered. 'Fish-heads not good enough for the likes of you – you mollycoddled—'

Brindle did not manage to finish – Sammy sprung at him with claws unsheathed. They grappled and rolled over together in the dust, spitting and biting, scratching for all they were worth. Brindle soon found that Sammy was no weakling. Although the young cat had no craft in his fighting, his sheer weight bore down on Brindle, pinning him underneath.

'No – titbits,' Sammy panted. 'Your own words. You – wanted – no titbits. And you think – I'll accept them – from you?'

Brindle snarled, but his breath came with difficulty. The larger cat was crushing him. Suddenly, on the fringe of the waste ground, the vagabonds were gathering, attracted by the noise. They watched the contest with interest. There was nothing they enjoyed so much as a good brawl. One of them, Brownie, detached herself from the group and came running across. Brindle was her brother. Sammy watched her out of the corner of his eye, but he did not slacken his grip. Before Brownie could join the fray the voice of Patch rang out.

'Keep away, Brownie! It's a fair fight. I want to see how this soft cat makes out.'

Pinkie was next to him. 'He seems to be making out very well,' she commented. 'Who would have thought it?'

'You've played – games with me – long enough,' Sammy hissed. 'You'll get no more of my food.'

'Brute might have other ideas,' Patch informed him. 'But I've no quarrel. You've bested Brindle all right. You could become quite a fighter in time.'

'Let him go,' snarled Brownie. 'He can scarcely breathe.'

Sammy heeded her and loosened his hold. At once Brindle leapt up, aimed a blow at his adversary's flank and dashed off. Sammy felt the claws rake through his flesh in a sharp rush of pain. He still had a lot to learn.

'A trick!' spat Sammy, as Brownie looked at him in triumph. But the young cat was not finished yet. He raced after Brindle who was running across Belinda's meadow. Now he found he had superior speed as well. He gained on the other tabby, pounced and bowled him over.

Brindle was badly winded. Before Sammy could press home his advantage once more, his opponent gasped out, 'All right, Sammy. You win.' His sides heaved as he fought for his breath. 'There's – no – contest.'

Sammy was victorious. He sat and watched Brindle with a look of smug satisfaction. Eventually the other cat recovered.

'You're right,' Brindle muttered. 'The arrangement wasn't fair. It was – never meant to be. We thought we could – make use of you and have – our fun as well. But you're not – such a fool, are you?'

'Not quite the one you took me for, no,' Sammy answered, without malice. 'I tell you what, Brindle. There's still a plateful of food untouched in my garden. Let's go shares.'

'Are you – serious?' Brindle asked incredulously.

'Yes. Why not? No hard feelings. You've been honest with me. I bear no grudges.'

'You're a generous sort,' Brindle remarked wonderingly. 'After all this. Well well. Perhaps we can learn something from you, too.'

'Of course you can. We can help each other. Come on then.' He led the old enemy away, now his new friend.

Through the gardens, over the fences, they went shoulder to shoulder. At the last fence Sammy went ahead. His mistress's garden was clear. He called to Brindle. They went over and up to the plate.

'I don't believe it,' murmured Sammy.

'Empty!' cried Brindle.

Yet there were crumbs of meat on the plate and they were fresh. As they stared in disappointment at this, they failed to notice Pinkie nimbly climbing the apple tree, with some choice lumps of food between her teeth.

Sammy's suspicions fell on Josephine but, whoever it was who had been there before them, there was no longer any reason to stay around. All at once Sammy remembered his hidden food supply.

'We shan't go hungry, after all,' he told his companion. 'Follow me.'

From the apple tree Pinkie waited for them to get well clear and then descended. She had to get back to Brute, but all the time she was thinking about Sammy. She was impressed by the way he had taken his stand against Brindle and then dealt with him. She already thought him a fine-looking animal, and had forgotten all about his strangely marked face. By comparison with the animals she had always mixed with, Sammy was such a healthy, fit-looking specimen. However, for now Brute was the cat that called the tune.

Sammy and Brindle arrived at the hedgerow bordering Belinda's field. There was no difficulty in locating the rabbit. They had both been able to smell it from some distance away.

'Did you catch this?' Brindle asked in astonishment.

'Er – in a way,' Sammy answered vaguely. 'I've had one good meal off it already. We can share the rest.'

Brindle was looking at Sammy's flank. The wound he had inflicted was quite visible. 'I'm afraid you're still bleeding,' he remarked awkwardly.

'My first scars,' Sammy answered. He seemed to be rather proud of them. 'Now I truly feel like one of you. And, Brindle, you didn't go scot-free either.'

'I didn't. You're a strong cat,' Brindle acknowledged. They ate their meal companionably. Then the vagabond cat said, 'You've proved yourself in two ways already, haven't you? Patch won't have to ask again. You can fight and you can hunt.'

'Hunt?' repeated Sammy. 'Oh, I see. Well, to be honest, I didn't actually hunt this rabbit.'

'But you caught it?'

'Well, I found it, you see,' Sammy admitted. 'But,' he added hastily, 'I was on my way to hunt. Where *you* go, you know – behind that tall fence.'

'I see now,' said Brindle. 'I suppose this animal was already dead when you found it. Well, *hunting* rabbits is not easy. It takes quite a time to learn the right moves. So the sooner we begin on that the better.'

'We? You mean you'll teach me?' Sammy asked excitedly.

'I can give you some help anyway,' said Brindle. 'Dusk is the best time for rabbits, so we'll get together at that time tomorrow.' He had assumed that Sammy was going back to his home now.

—11—

New Ways

Sammy could not make up his mind whether to go or stay. He wanted to make a full commitment to his new way of life, but the comfort and familiarity of the shed where he had been born was still a powerful magnet to him. He decided to sleep in the shed once more and make his plans known to Stella. Then he would leave and become one of the vagabonds in Quartermile Field, with all that that entailed. His old mistress would soon cease to try and tempt him back, for the food she believed he had been eating would from now on stay on the plate. The so-called exchange of food with the other cats had ended this night. He spoke to Brindle.

'I'll meet you at the tall fence as the light fades.'

'I shall be there,' the other tabby replied.

'I hope we can continue to be friends,' said Sammy.

'So do I. And don't mind Brownie, my sister. She did what she did to help me. It's understandable, isn't it? And it didn't save me.'

'I understand that,' agreed Sammy, though he wondered if Josephine would have acted in the same way. 'But there are many things I don't understand yet about your ways.'

Brindle and Sammy separated. Back in the shed Sammy asked Josephine about the empty plate. She denied eating two meals, saying that she never touched her brother's food. So for Sammy the mystery remained.

Stella awoke and said, rather irritably, 'I wonder you come back here at all, Sammy, if you only come here to sleep.'

'I've come for the last time,' he told his mother. 'I wanted to make my farewells to you both. I don't expect I shall see you again.'

'Don't do us any favours,' Josephine answered. 'You're not one of us any more. You smell different, you move differently, you're half-wild already.'

'All right, Josephine,' said Stella. 'Sammy's not answerable to you.' She turned to her son. 'It was thoughtful of you to do this. I know you have a heart. But, Sammy, you're making a mistake. The excitement you think you're going to find will not make up for the misery of cold and hunger and friendlessness which you're going to experience. I know you want to be like your father. But you weren't born into his way of life and you'll find it much more difficult to try and acquire it.'

'I shall have friends,' Sammy asserted.

'No, Sammy. Not the fond, kindly sort of friends you've known up to now. These will be friends while all goes well, and when it doesn't they will be rivals and even enemies. But I know it's no use warning you. You didn't listen before, nor did I really expect you to. And you won't listen now. Just remember, though, that where you're going we'll be unable to help you. You'll have to rely on yourself alone.'

'I mean to do so,' Sammy told her. 'I'm not frightened of that. What is there for me here? An endless round of uneventful days filled with the same routine. No new faces, no needs to cater for.'

'Yes,' said Stella, 'that's not enough for a son of Beau. I know and I've always known. You're part of him and, when you meet, you might find you have too much in common.'

Sammy reflected on that, but he was not yet equipped to interpret the remark. He began to wash himself. The conversation was at an end. It was strange for him as he settled himself, tucking his paws under his chest, to think that this was the last time he would lie here, in his birthplace.

High up in one of the wooden struts of the shed, Tiptoe was waiting. These days he stayed well out of reach and spent as little time as possible on the ground. And he was tiring of it. That was why he was waiting until it would be safe to talk to Sammy.

Stella and Josephine were curled up together as usual. Sammy also was napping but he heard Tiptoe's squeaks. At first he could not see him.

'I'm above your head,' said the mouse. 'I'm spending my life up in the air. I feel if I can't come down to earth more often, I might change into a bird!'

'Whatever are you babbling about?' Sammy hissed.

'Those wild animals you've invited on to my doorstep! How long must we mice live like this? Food's hard to come by at these heights.'

Sammy understood and was more amused than contrite. But he did not let the mouse see this. 'Your worries are over, Tiptoe,' he assured the little animal. 'There will be no more strangers coming into the garden.'

'Is that a promise?'

'The arrangement about the food is over,' Sammy said. 'I'm leaving this place for good.'

'Oh,' said Tiptoe. 'I wasn't expecting that. Where are you going?'

'To a new area,' the young tabby answered. He was not going to admit to Quartermile Field.

But the mouse was no fool. He guessed at once where

Sammy was heading. 'So you're going to join the creatures who've been thieving your mistress's food?' he
squeaked in indignation. 'I've seen them, one by one.
Black and ginger and white.'

'White?'

'A white one came tonight and then climbed up the
tree,' shrilled the mouse. 'Don't pretend you don't know.
You've encouraged them.'

Sammy had the answer now. It was Pinkie who had
taken advantage of himself and Brindle while they had
been squabbling. This was the way of things in the vagabond world. He turned back to Tiptoe.

'You're a fine one to talk about thieving,' he chuckled.
'You and your friends spend your whole lives doing
it.'

'Of course we do,' said Tiptoe. 'Tee hee.' He saw the
funny side of it too. 'But what we take isn't missed and, in
any case, it's expected of us.' He tittered again. Then he
said, more soberly, 'I suppose our paths won't cross
for a while?'

'I suppose not,' Sammy replied, 'though I should be
sorry not to see you again. You're a comical little fellow
and I like you a lot. Perhaps we could meet—'

'No,' Tiptoe interrupted firmly. 'We couldn't. I don't
travel to those regions.'

'I understand.'

'But I think you'll be back one day, despite what you
say,' the mouse said firmly. 'I'm sure you're not cut out to
mingle with those cat tramps.'

'Everyone thinks that,' Sammy said blithely. 'I don't
care. I shall prove you wrong.'

'Maybe. But Sammy, will you give me your word? I
have to know that it's safe for me to come to ground.'

'I'll make sure it is; don't worry. No animal will come
here if there's no food to be had.'

'Good. I'll trust you, then.'

'I hope you will.'

'Well – good luck.'

'Good luck, Tiptoe.'

In the morning, Sammy stayed on in the shed whilst his mother and sister roamed the garden. He wanted dearly to show his affection for the last time to his good mistress, but he thought her kind words and caresses would make him regretful at leaving her. And there was always the chance that she might shut him in, after his recent absences, to prevent his wandering off again.

Later, Molly's grizzled nose sniffed at the shed door. She came in, wagging her tattered old tail.

'Oh Molly,' Sammy said softly, 'you're the one friend I shall miss most of all.'

'I feel the same about you,' she murmured.

'I – I'll never forget you.'

'Of course not – nor any of us here,' said Molly. 'And Sammy, don't be afraid to come back here. It'll always be your real home. Our mistress will always be—'

'I know,' Sammy broke in quickly. 'You think I'm making a mistake. But I have to do this, you see. I can't help myself. It's in my blood.'

'Yes. But, let me caution you. Watch out for B – Beau. He's a jealous, proud creature. And he won't know who you are.'

'We'll get along, I'm sure, if we ever do meet,' Sammy said confidently.

Molly looked at him long and hard. She seemed to be on the point of saying more, but gave him a loving lick instead across his crossed-out face, and then waddled sadly away. Sammy almost wavered. Then he steeled himself, ran out of the shed and up, over the fence and away.

Behind his back as he ran on the cockerel called out: 'Run, run, run. But you can't fly!'

Sammy made himself comfortable in the hedgerow where he had devoured the rabbit with Brindle. As the late August sun dipped towards the horizon, he stirred. Now Quartermile Field beckoned. Sammy went slowly across Belinda's meadow. The goat watched him but gave no greeting. The cat reached the road and waited for the passing vehicles to disappear. He ran nimbly across and was at the bomb site at once, threading his way through the vegetation. He traversed the waste ground, remembering the route to the tall wire fence which Pinkie had shown him. The high wire mesh fence reared up in front of him, and Sammy looked for the way through. He found the hole and glanced round for Brindle. He had not yet come but dusk was closing in.

Sammy decided to get on the right side of the wire, amongst the wild cabbage and other vegetable plants. He wanted to see the rabbits coming. He soon noticed Pinkie was there before him, lying low. She ignored him. Brute was there too. Sammy guessed the other cats were dotted about the place, all in hiding. He wondered where Brindle was.

From the far end of the old allotments, where they adjoined open country, Sammy noticed some movement. A group of some dozen or so rabbits, of various sizes, were spilling into the area in fits and starts. They stopped often to check all around for safety, their ceaselessly twitching noses working hard to identify every scent. They came on, closer, closer. . . . A large one, accompanied by a youngster, paused by a cabbage plant. . . .

Brute shot from cover and pinned the adult rabbit to the ground. The cat's muscular shoulders produced a grip from his front paws like a vice. Almost at the same instant the youngster was easily caught by Pinkie. Sammy saw the remaining rabbits scatter. They dashed away in all directions, their white powder-puffs of tails showing vividly in the early evening light. Now the other cats showed themselves as they raced in pursuit. Sammy realized that if he himself did not move at once his chance would be lost. He singled out the nearest animal and bolted after it. But he was a mere novice in the knowledge of rabbits' ways. He was no match for the animal's speed or tactics. Its zigzagging course confused him and when he stopped to look about him, all of the uncaught rabbits had disappeared.

Pinkie and Brute had soon despatched their victims and were beginning to drag them away to cover. Sammy felt rather foolish at his failure, but he swallowed his pride and ambled toward the cats with a contrived air of nonchalance. Brute dropped his prey and sprang out at Sammy, lashing out with his claws. His right forepaw seared a path through Sammy's face fur, narrowly missing one eye. It was a vicious scratch and the young tabby fell back in consternation. His face smarted acutely.

'Don't think to come begging to us,' snarled his attacker.

'I'd no such intention,' Sammy protested. 'But you didn't wait to find out.'

'I don't believe in waiting,' Brute rasped. 'Waiting's a fool's game.'

All this time Pinkie remained silent. She continued about her business of removing her quarry.

'You'll have to learn a better set of moves if you don't mean to starve,' Brute scoffed.

'I shall,' said Sammy. 'Brindle is going to help me.'

'Help?' Brute echoed mockingly. 'I think you're mis-

taken. It's each cat for himself here and devil take the
hindmost. That's our philosophy and you'd better adopt
it, if you mean to live like us.'

The other cats were beginning to gather around. Some
had been lucky in the hunt – some had not. Sammy was
conscious that Brindle was not amongst them.

Now Pinkie spoke up. 'Sammy is a fine-looking cat.
But he's not up to our tricks yet.'

'No, nor will he be,' grunted Brute. 'Cats brought up in
soft ways don't make good hunters.'

Sammy felt the uncomfortable truth of this. He went
on the defensive. 'When a cat's forced to learn new ways,
he must. Mustn't he?' he added hesitantly.

'He must, mustn't he?' Brute mimicked him sarcastically. 'Unless he starves himself first.'

'I think he'll look after himself all right,' said Patch. 'He
can fight, anyway – we've seen that.' He was not
afraid of Brute.

'I've seen nothing,' Brute growled. Then he turned
sharply to Sammy again. He was reminded of something.
'I'm told you've decided your rich pet food is no longer
on offer to the animals here.' He spat the word 'pet'. 'By
what authority?'

Sunny answered for him. 'He turned up his nose at
what we offered in exchange. Said it was unfair.'

'Is this correct?' Brute snapped.

'Yes,' said Sammy. 'You vagabonds took advantage
of me.'

Brute stared at him. '*We* took advantage of *you*?' he
whispered. 'But you are the one with all the advantages,
my soft friend.' There was a menace in his words.

'Not any more,' returned Sammy stoutly. 'I've left
them all behind.'

Pinkie chipped in. 'Who eats your food now?'

'There will be no food if I don't return.'

'And what of tonight?' Brute rasped. 'Is there good rich food going to waste?'

'Mottle is on her way to eat it,' Sunny said.

'Then I'll stop her,' Sammy declared. He remembered his vow to Tiptoe, but said, 'My old mistress must not be fooled any longer. The arrangement's over.'

'Is it now?' Brute hissed. 'Well, you'd better go and see about it then, hadn't you?' As soon as the words were out of his mouth, he rushed to the hole in the wire fence through which Sammy had passed, and lay across it. Sunny the ginger cat, who disliked Sammy, took up his station at another gap.

'It seems your way out is blocked,' Pinkie murmured. She was excited by the threat of a conflict and longed to see what Sammy would do.

The young tabby was angry and determined Tiptoe should not be put at risk by a failure on his part. He looked at the towering wire fence. It was a daunting barrier but he knew he had to scale it. There was one thing in his favour. An elder tree grew close on the other side. If he could pull himself up to the top of the fence, he could jump from there on to the top branches of the elder and so climb down that way. Brute and Sunny waited. Pinkie, Patch and Brownie watched the new-comer. Only Brindle and Mottle, the tortoiseshell and white, were missing, and Scruff, who could not hunt rabbits. Sammy calculated his chances. Whatever the result should be, he knew he had to attempt the climb.

He ran at the fence and leapt on to it. The wire whipped back and forth. When it stilled he started to haul himself up, using the power of his shoulders and putting his paws through the holes while gripping the links with his claws. He mounted steadily and presently arrived at the top. Now he had the more difficult job of heaving himself over to prepare for his leap. He gathered his feet together under him. The fence rippled alarmingly. Sammy felt himself overbalancing but, at the last moment, he sprang out wildly and landed awkwardly, but safely, on the elder tree.

'He can climb too,' Patch muttered.

'He *can* climb,' Pinkie echoed emphatically.

But Sammy did not linger to hear her praise. He scrambled down the tree and raced off to intercept Mottle. He could not know that she had already entered Mrs Lambert's garden.

Quartermile Field

Sunny was annoyed that Brute had allowed Sammy to get away. 'You could have stopped him easily,' he said in a flattering tone.

'Of course I could,' Brute answered. 'But he earned his passage.' There was a grudging respect in his voice. Sunny noticed it and disliked Sammy the more.

'The time hasn't yet come,' Brute went on, 'when Sammy and I will have to face each other.'

The other cats marked his words, knowing full well what they meant. Pinkie felt a fresh thrill of excitement tingling in her veins at the prospect. Brute returned to his prey.

On the other side of the fence, deeply hidden in the rank weeds, Brindle had watched and heard everything. Brute's appearance on the scene had driven him into hiding. He had not dared to appear as Sammy's comrade in the King Cat's sight. But comrade he was in his heart. And, after this latest scene, the 'soft' young tabby was fast becoming his hero. None of the vagabond cats, not even Brute, had ever climbed that fence.

Sammy ran on, desperately hoping Tiptoe was not in one of his adventurous moods. His concern so absorbed him that he narrowly missed being hit by a bicycle as he sprinted across the road. A din broke out before he had got much farther on his way, and it was a din emanating from one of the gardens. A dog's barks and a sound of squabbling angry cats rent the air. Sammy thought he recognized those rather wheezy barks.

A short time later he saw Mottle, the tortoiseshell and white female, running towards him fearfully. She did not heed him and would have passed him by.

'Stop!' cried Sammy. 'What happened?' He had to know.

Mottle skidded to a halt and panted, 'So – it's you. I only just escaped.' She seemed to think Sammy was to blame. Then she explained. 'I went for the food and was attacked by two cats and a great black dog. Why weren't you there?'

Sammy could see what had happened. In his absence, Mottle had not checked if the garden was empty before rushing in. She had not known, or had forgotten, about the other animals who shared his old home.

'You know why I wasn't there,' he told her. 'You saw my fight with Brindle. You shouldn't have gone.'

'I wish I hadn't,' she snapped. 'The dog might have killed me.'

'No,' said Sammy. 'She wouldn't have done that. She's not savage. She merely wanted to frighten you off. You don't belong there.'

'No, and I'm thankful for it,' was Mottle's retort. To the vagabond cats, dogs were their fiercest enemies.

'Come on,' Sammy said with some sympathy, 'I'll walk back with you.'

A scared look returned to the female cat's eyes. 'Back – where?' she whispered.

'To Quartermile Field, of course.'

Now Mottle was puzzled. 'But I thought—'

'Never mind what you thought,' Sammy interrupted. 'My home is now the same as yours.'

As they travelled, Sammy thought again about Tiptoe. He was no longer alarmed about the mouse, for he knew he never appeared when Stella and Josephine were about. In the waste ground, Sammy left Mottle to go her own way. He himself went back to the old allotment area. He was hoping to find some rabbit meat left from the vagabonds' hunt. What he did find was Scruff there before him. The lame cat regularly searched for the others' leavings. He eyed Sammy suspiciously.

'There's not enough for one here,' he growled, 'let alone two of us.'

'Not even a mouthful?' Sammy suggested.

'No.' Scruff's eyes wandered over the tabby's stocky body. 'It won't hurt you to go without food for once anyway. My whole life is one of going without.'

Sammy knew this was an exaggeration, but there was some justice in the lame cat's remarks. However, it would not do to seem too agreeable. He was part of the vagabond world now and had to vie with all of the cats. He simply replied, 'You were first here on this occasion, but next time will be different.'

Sammy turned and sauntered away. He did not want to take food out of the lame cat's mouth but he intended it to be known that he would not be taken for granted.

He headed for the spot where Pinkie had told him there were mouse-holes. Mice as food were no real substitute for rabbits, but he had to work up to that sort of thing. He must set his sights a little lower for now.

He made his way to the tree stump near the grassy bank and flattened himself behind it. His dilated pupils raked the slope for signs of life. Nothing moved. No matter. He might not be a skilful hunter as yet, but he had patience. He turned his head once to see if he were being observed. No other cat seemed to be nearby. As he looked away again, he caught, out of the corner of an eye, a scurry of movement. He jerked his head round, at the same time pressing himself even closer against the ground. A plump little mouse was sitting by one of the holes, grooming itself. Sammy launched himself forward with great speed.

Of course he should have waited a little. The mouse had been too close to its bolt-hole. Despite his swiftness, Sammy was left scrabbling bare earth after he pounced. The mouse was safe. Furious, frustrated, Sammy dug a paw into the hole and scratched frantically around. Not a whisker could he find. He was glad there were no witnesses of his second failure. He sat on his haunches and licked his lips. The pain from Brute's scratch made his face throb. Sammy was angry and disgusted with himself. His first attempts at hunting had been a disaster. He did not remain to see if any other mice should emerge. He turned his back on the bank and came face to face with Brindle.

'Oh!' said Sammy.

'I – er – I'm sorry about our rendezvous,' Brindle said awkwardly. 'Brute, you see.'

Sammy understood. 'I'm not having any success,' he confessed. 'I can't catch mice either.'

'No. It takes a time to learn their ways,' Brindle answered. 'I watched you with the rabbits. I can give you some tips for next time; tell you where you went wrong. But now—'

'Yes?'

'Pinkie sent me.'

'Sent you?' cried Sammy. 'Pinkie? What do you mean?'

'She seems very taken with your climbing display,' Brindle informed him. 'Says you deserve not to go hungry. Brute's out of the way for the moment and – well, Pinkie saved something for you.'

Sammy perked up at once. 'Things are looking up,' he commented. 'Where is she?'

'In her shelter.'

'Are you coming?'

'I don't think I'm expected to. It's you she's inviting.'

'Oh,' said Sammy. 'How did she know where to find me?'

'She didn't, but she knew I was looking for you.'

'Thanks, Brindle. I'll go.' Sammy was about to trot away, then he hesitated. 'When do the rabbiting lessons begin?' he queried.

'Whenever you want. When we next see each other,' Brindle answered.

Sammy left him and sought out the dilapidated old hut where Pinkie sheltered. On his way he imagined the tasty rabbit pieces he was going to eat that the little white female had reserved for him. Pinkie was waiting for him. Without a word she led him to the food. Sammy stared at it.

'What is this?' he faltered.

'Can't you see?' asked Pinkie.

'It's . . . it's not rabbit,' he muttered disappointedly.

'Of course it isn't rabbit,' she snapped. 'You didn't catch any.'

Sammy looked at her sharply. 'Is this a joke?' he murmured. 'Because if it is—'

'I don't know what you mean,' Pinkie replied. 'I told you of the old woman who sometimes leaves titbits for us here. Well, here are some. I've left them for you. Brute and I have eaten enough.'

'Have you indeed?' Sammy said slowly. His anger was kindling. 'So this is all I was invited to, is it?'

'Well, you don't think the King Cat is likely to share the prey he himself catches, do you?' Pinkie returned scathingly. Sammy was irritating her.

'Only with you, his favourite, I suppose,' Sammy answered in an icy whisper. His disappointment prevented his recognition of Pinkie's intended friendliness.

'I caught my own meal,' she answered. 'So did many of the others. You're a great climber but a pathetic hunter.'

'Not for long,' Sammy hissed at her. 'I'll soon be a great hunter too. As for these morsels of – of – nothing,' he spluttered, indicating the scraps, 'they're fit only for the likes of Scruff!'

'You're very snooty, Sammy,' Pinkie told him coldly. 'I meant it for the best. You're not used to finding your own food. If you were, you'd see these for what they are – the difference between life and death, on occasion.'

Sammy looked at her steadily. He was mollified. His temper cooled. 'I'm sorry,' he said. 'I misjudged you. I thought you were mocking me.' He examined the stale meat and fish-heads their human well-wisher had brought. Suddenly he realized with great clarity the change in his life and the new dimensions of it. There *was not* anything better than this for vagabonds, and he was a vagabond; a vagabond who could not hunt. Sammy was humbled. He bent his head and ate.

Pinkie watched him silently. They did not speak to each other again; both were aware of a presence. Brute had returned and was regarding them together.

'A cosy scene,' he declared, padding into sight. 'You won't be thinking of sharing our quarters too?' He posed the question to Sammy sarcastically.

'No,' mumbled the young male, gulping his mouthful. 'I don't go where I'm not wanted.'

'Hurry up,' Pinkie urged him. 'You linger.'

Sammy ate no more of the ill-tasting food. He left without further comment, marvelling over Pinkie's ambivalence towards him. When Brute was away, she would extend a sort of friendship. But when he was around . . . well, it was quite another matter.

Over the next few days, from time to time Sammy thought he could hear his old mistress calling him. Her voice penetrated to the new tough world he had made his home. Quartermile Field was not so very distant from Mrs Lambert's garden after all. But now the sound of her voice had become like the last echo from his old life. Sammy was fully occupied with the urgent need to improve his hunting ability. With Brindle's help and his own determination he had begun to have some success.

He had learnt how to catch mice and voles. They were easy enough once you realized that you had to wait for them to move beyond their escape routes before you pounced. Now Sammy watched the rabbits whenever they appeared, noting the pattern of their movements and their variations of pace. He had steadily lost weight, confined to his diet of mice and the like. Now he was not very much stouter than the other vagabond cats. His luck in finding the rabbit carcass in the road was not repeated, although he went daily to look for one.

Brindle asked him, 'Why don't you try again to catch one?'

'When I'm ready, I will,' Sammy answered. He was afraid of failing again in front of Brute, who had begun to treat him with a little more respect. In fact Sammy had found a sort of acceptance amongst the vagabonds who no longer referred to his softness or his ugly face. Most of them ignored him, as they ignored each other while they went about their own business. Brindle was his friend and Brindle's sister, Brownie, had changed towards him because of this. Only Sunny, the ginger cat, continued to harbour any real resentment. He saw Sammy as a threat to his chance of becoming the King Cat when Brute's days were over. Not that there was any sign of that at the present. Brute was still well and truly in control.

Sammy grew thinner and harder. Stella and Josephine would scarcely have recognized him. Sammy never thought about his relatives, but he did occasionally recall Molly and still with a pang. As for Tiptoe, perhaps it was just as well he was not called to mind. . . .

Eventually Sammy felt sufficiently confident to stalk rabbits again. He lay amongst the remnants of the cabbage and lettuce plants while it was barely dusk. If the rabbits were coming, he wanted to be the first to know. But the vagabonds began to arrive before the rabbits. Sammy noticed Pinkie was on her own. She approached him deliberately.

'Brute's on his travels again,' she announced, as if she were well aware this would be of interest to him.

Sammy felt himself relaxing. 'Where does he go?' he asked, though he did not really care.

'Who knows? Nobody asks him.' Pinkie crouched down by Sammy's side.

'I hope your face has healed well,' she said.

'I've forgotten about it,' he lied.

'We can still be friends,' Pinkie offered. 'It's quite natural for us to get along, isn't it?'

Sammy looked at the little white cat penetratingly. There seemed to be a suggestion, even an invitation, somewhere at the back of her words. 'I'd like that,' he said. Pinkie had a definite attraction for him and he was a little flattered by her singling him out.

'I'd like it too,' she responded coyly.

'Brute's the drawback,' Sammy muttered.

'Let him do as he chooses,' Pinkie retorted. 'He doesn't rule me.'

'Not when he's absent, no,' Sammy remarked subtly.

'Pinkie said nothing, though she felt the irony. She had noticed a group of rabbits loping into the area.

There was little breeze so the scent of the cats was not easy to pick up. The rabbits paused as they usually did, listening and smelling and looking around for all they were worth. Now Sammy was all agog. His tail flicked nervously. He singled out one of the smaller animals from the band for the attack. The rabbits came on. It was now or never. Sammy dashed out at them at full speed. His victim could not have seen him before he was on it, and crushed it under him. He copied what he had seen of Brute's action before and made short work of the animal. The rest of the rabbits were put to flight. They ran helter-skelter for safety, making it impossible for the other cats to have any chance of catching them.

Sammy proudly dragged back his trophy. But there was trouble in store for him. The vagabonds rounded on him, saying he had spoilt their sport. Sammy dropped his rabbit.

'You should have been quicker,' he told them defensively.

'What chance was there when you dashed out so early?' Sunny snapped.

'Speed is the essence of success in hunting, isn't it?' Sammy reminded him. 'You could have been the first but I beat you to it.'

The other cats quietened down, sensing that Sunny might decide to fight.

'I don't need any lessons from you,' the ginger cat snarled. 'You know such a lot, don't you?'

The old cat Patch, the former leader, could not resist

pointing out, 'He seems to have learnt how to beat you to the strike, Sunny.'

The vagabonds were amused. Pinkie's eyes were huge as she looked from Sammy to his antagonist. She longed for a brawl where the tabby would emerge victorious, stronger and bolder than ever. Sunny growled low down in his throat. His tail swished a warning and he took a few stiff steps forward, his gaze fixed on Sammy.

'You take offence easily,' Sammy said lightly. He thought he had the measure of the ginger and was not cowed. 'This is my first success with a rabbit. You have caught many in your time, I don't doubt. How can you begrudge me this one?'

'Simple,' Sunny spat. 'The rabbits will not be back for a while and I shall go hungry because of you.'

Pinkie could see the situation in danger of cooling off. So she quite deliberately fanned the flames. 'Sammy might leave you a titbit or so,' she murmured derogatorily.

Her words had the required effect. 'We'll see if we can do better than that,' hissed the ginger cat. Then, instead of launching himself at Sammy, he snatched up the dead rabbit and made off with it. Sammy was so astonished at the move that he failed to react at once.

'Where's your speed now?' Pinkie urged him.

Sunny had not got far, hampered by the weight of the animal. Sammy ran after him and seized the other end of the carcass where it dangled from the ginger's jaws. Each cat tugged with all his strength, trying to wrest it away from the other. Pinkie trotted up to see the outcome. Sunny tried to twist the rabbit away; then he shook it vigorously. But Sammy held fast. Now their stamina was put to the test as each cat determined to outlast his foe, using his shoulder, neck and foreleg muscles in the struggle. After a bit, it became apparent that Sunny was weakening. Sammy's prior claim to the prey gave him an added incentive in the battle and, in any case, he was naturally fitter. He sensed he had the advantage, exerted a final ounce of strength, and jerked his quarry free from his adversary.

Sunny stood panting. 'You'll – regret – this,' he gasped.

'Will I?' Sammy replied easily. 'Don't count on it.' He felt brimful of confidence. With a swagger he picked up the rabbit again and walked off without a backward glance. He knew perfectly well the ginger cat could do nothing now. Pinkie followed gleefully in his wake.

Sammy started to look for a secluded spot to eat in.

'I have just the place for us,' Pinkie offered.

Sammy was intrigued by the 'us'.

'In my hut.' She took the lead.

When they reached it Sammy deposited his burden inside on the broken floor. 'You're quite sure Brute won't return?' he asked. 'He'd see me as an intruder.'

'I don't think we'll see him for a time, though with Brute you can never be sure,' Pinkie said. 'But why should you worry? You're a hunter and a fighter.'

'I'm not a match for Brute,' Sammy answered honestly, yet even as he said it he knew there would come a day soon when he would have to be, or accept the consequences.

Pinkie looked at him strangely. 'Do you still wonder about your father?' she asked.

'My—' Sammy began, then realized he had not thought about him for a long time.

'I think you've forgotten him,' Pinkie concluded. 'So I'll say nothing for the moment. But I may have something to tell you at another time, if you wish.'

Sammy regarded her pensively.

'Come on,' she said, 'let's eat.'

—13—

Beau

Soon Sammy felt that life in and around Quartermile Field suited him. Pinkie was his constant companion. The other cats noticed this and saw the newcomer in a different light. He had become an animal to be reckoned with. Sammy's attitude to them had changed too. The friendliness in him which had been developed while he was still a pet had been replaced by something more akin to a simple tolerance of those that shared the same territory. He did not go out of his way to attract their company, not even Brindle's, though he did have a warmer feeling for him than the rest. Sammy was very much in command of his own life now. He had developed a strategy of his own when hunting rabbits which usually proved successful. But he was always aware that he was competing with the other vagabonds for food and made sure he played fair. He was quite simply the swiftest and strongest of all of them – that is, as long as Brute was not around. As for Sunny, he had not dared to approach Sammy again. He knew he had no hope of defeating him unless he could catch him in a moment of weakness or when he was at some other disadvantage.

Sammy had begun to explore farther. He roamed the open countryside where it bordered the bomb site and one day Brindle took him to a shallow stream. Here sometimes little fish swam too close to the bank and could be hooked out, if a cat used his paw quickly enough. Sammy practised his fishing technique. The fish were too small to make much of a meal, but he enjoyed the sport of using eye, paw and speed in what could be a very satisfying combination. He shared whatever he managed to catch – rabbit, mouse, vole or fish – with Pinkie. In return he had the benefit of a dry, warm shelter when he needed it, and this was very useful now autumn had begun, bringing with it colder, wetter weather.

But he had to be aware that this arrangement was only a temporary one. Brute would return and Sammy would give ground or fight. Pinkie knew this too and relished the prospect. She wanted Sammy to fight for her. Whatever happened she knew she would still be the favourite of either champion, be it Brute or Sammy. And she wanted nothing less than the King Cat for her consort, though she could not have admitted to any preference because as yet she did not herself realize that she had one.

Meanwhile Brute was discovering he had something to contend with that he had not expected. He had made a slow circuit of the area with which he was familiar. He ranged farther than any of the vagabonds. He was the leader and he really felt that this wide stretch of country was his domain. He never went close to human habitations but, at the end of his circuit, he brought himself once more to the meadow of Belinda the goat. Belinda recognized him and he recognized her, but they held no conversation.

Brute pushed himself through the dying grasses towards the hedgerow. Occasionally he called in his harsh voice, as he had done periodically throughout his wanderings. This was his personal signal, his statement to any creature who might be listening that he, Brute, was on his rounds. The vegetation was wet and glistened in the evening light. Brute's fur was soaked but he cared nothing for that. At the end of Belinda's field he found Stella waiting for him.

'Hello, Beau,' she greeted him in her usual admiring way.

'Stella,' he answered fondly, and in a far warmer tone than any of the vagabonds had ever heard, Pinkie included.

'I heard you calling a long way back. I knew I would meet you here.'

Brute appreciated her loyalty and affection. Stella was different. He liked her refined manner and her general air of contentment. To her and other female cats under his spell he was no brute. He was a rakish and handsome specimen and they had a different name for him because they saw him differently. But if Brute had a special favourite, it was probably Stella.

'Have you travelled far?' she murmured as she looked at him with her steady, confident gaze.

'Far and wide,' he answered. 'And how pleasing to find you at the end.'

'You flatter me,' she said. 'Of course, you always have.'

'You're a cat to *be* flattered,' Brute returned gallantly. 'Is your life as comfortable as ever?'

'It doesn't change,' Stella replied, 'except we all grow older. I no longer have kittens. I have a mature daughter who is my friend and an inquisitive son who has left me to make his own life in another part.'

Brute was interested. 'Has he?' he mused. 'How does he manage on his own? Does he beg from humans?'

'I don't know,' Stella answered. 'He has his own ideas of what a male cat should be and do. He was very eager to meet his father, though I held him back as long as I could.'

'Meet me?' Brute asked in astonishment. 'Why, no, I—

I – have no part to play with those I've fathered.'

'He's very like you in some ways,' Stella said.

'Is he?' Brute was intrigued despite himself. 'In what way?'

'Oh, your wandering spirit and some of your dash,' he was told. 'There's no doubt which of his parents he favours most. And he's a tabby too.'

'Well. And what do you call him?'

'Sammy.'

'Sammy!' Brute cried in a startled way. 'So that's it,' he muttered. 'Yes – I can see it now.'

'What are you saying?'

'I know him, Stella. I know Sammy. But I didn't know him for my son.'

'But – but – what do you mean, Beau?'

'It's all quite simple,' he replied. 'He's taken up residence around Quartermile Field with the other roamers who pay court to me. They know me as Brute so, naturally, he hasn't discovered who I am.'

'In all this while?' Stella asked incredulously. 'Do none of them call you Beau?'

'There is – er – just one, yes,' Brute admitted. 'But she only does so if we're alone.'

Stella said, 'Sammy wasn't born to your way of life, although I guessed one day he would be tempted to try to emulate you. Please, Beau, do what you can to make him come back to his proper home, before he suffers too much.'

'He's not suffering, Stella,' said Brute. 'In fact, he seems to be doing quite well.' Surprisingly, there was a note of pride in his voice. 'But I'll do what I can for you. It may be he's not cut out to tackle winter conditions like we vagabonds have to.'

'He isn't,' said Stella. 'He doesn't know what a winter is.'

'Well, I don't think our son will take kindly to your

idea,' Brute went on. 'So there will be only one way open to me and that'll be to drive him out by some means.'

Stella began to rub herself against Brute's chest and legs, brushing his face with her whiskers as she nuzzled him. If he needed any persuasion to do as she wished she was not slow to provide it. The two fond friends, from such different worlds, purred contentedly together. Stella's was a low, quiet purr and Brute's a harsh, noisy purr which almost carried to the ears of Belinda; yet both noises signified the same thing – their great pleasure in each other.

When Brute left Sammy's mother his head was full of the problem facing him – how to drive Sammy back to her. He stalked back to Quartermile Field, staring straight ahead but seeing nothing; lost in his thoughts. He did not want to fight his own son, and he could not decide whether to reveal his identity to Sammy or not. He did not know how Sammy would react. In the end it seemed best to Brute not to do so for the present. His mind started working on the notion of setting Sammy some sort of test. The passing of this test would be almost an impossibility, but Sammy would be told that it must be passed before he could be accepted fully into the community of the vagabond cats.

Brindle was the first to see Brute approaching. It was early morning. He hastened to the broken-down hut to alert Sammy. However, Pinkie forestalled him. She guessed the reason for Brindle's appearance and was determined that the long-desired confrontation should take place.

'Sammy's sleeping,' she told his friend, halting him outside.

'Yes, yes,' Brindle said quickly. 'We must wake him. Brute's back.'

'Does it matter?' Pinkie mewed silkily. 'He may not be

coming here straight away. Why should Sammy be disturbed?'

Brindle was no fool and could see that Pinkie meant to delay him. 'I know what you're after,' he said. 'Why provoke trouble between them?' He ran past her into the shelter.

'It'll come anyway,' Pinkie called after him. 'You can't stop it.'

Sammy was already wakened by the noise. He looked up at Brindle.

'Quickly – out,' said Brindle but, even as he turned, Brute's face appeared at the entrance. Behind him, Pinkie peered in, trembling with excitement.

Sammy jumped up guiltily, then cursed himself inwardly for this instinctive reaction.

Despite the new position he now found himself in with respect to the young tabby, Brute was angry and even jealous at what he saw. He knew at once Sammy and Pinkie had been consorting in his absence.

'So sorry to disturb you in your comfortable surroundings,' he said sarcastically.

'I – I'm going at once,' Sammy replied. Brindle had already vanished.

'Oh, but why?' Brute continued in the same tone. 'You seem so at home here.'

Sammy was quite prepared to give way and was about to slink past the King Cat, but this was not what Pinkie wanted. She intervened.

'I invited Sammy here,' she said coolly. 'I wanted him to share our shelter.' She knew she was exacerbating the situation and indeed meant to do so. Brute glowered at her, then turned to his son.

'Well, Sammy,' he said evenly, 'so you've made yourself a contender for the small advantages enjoyed by a King Cat?'

'No, no,' Sammy denied this. 'That wasn't my intention. You see, I—'

'Nevertheless,' rasped Brute, drowning him out, 'that's what you've done. Very well; there's something you should understand. These advantages have to be won, not taken for granted. I had to exert myself to reach the position of eminence around here. I'm not aware that you've done anything so far to merit it.'

'Sammy's become a great hunter,' Pinkie informed him, 'and a fighter too.'

'Has he indeed?' Brute returned. 'Well, he'll certainly need all his hunting and fighting skills from now on. And how interesting that he should have such a loyal supporter. You see, Sammy—' he turned again to his son and rival '— you can't expect to survive here without proving to me, and all of the vagabonds, that you'll be able to cope with the harsh conditions of winter. To my mind, you haven't yet shed completely the cloak of domesticity. Now, it would hardly be fair, would it, for you to become a burden on us all at the moment we, too, are finding life that much more of a struggle? So I'll tell you what's got to be, because I think it's safe to say I still call the tune around here until I'm shown otherwise.'

Brute paused. Sammy awaited his fate. And Pinkie suddenly realized, beyond any question, where her heart lay.

'You must undergo a test of endurance,' Brute went on, 'if you wish to stay in this part of the world. If you emerge from the test successfully we shall then all know that you're able to look after yourself in any straits or circumstances, without having to come cadging for assistance. Now, as a pet animal, you will be hard put to it to meet this challenge. If you do, all well and good, and you will emerge with credit. Then you and I will have to take our chances as they come. I think you understand me?' The older cat's eyes narrowed. Sammy was left in no doubt what he was hinting at. But now he was on his mettle.

'What is this test?' he asked boldly. Pinkie glowed.

'Firstly,' pronounced Brute, who was obliged to invent the requirements as he went on, 'you must go without food for a considerable period, except for any carrion or scraps you can find. Catching live prey will not be allowed because the purpose is to accustom you to the prevailing conditions of a normal winter. Then when your strength is at its lowest ebb, you will have to turn hunter again, catch an adult rabbit, kill it and fight one of the other cats (whom I shall nominate) for its possession. If you are the victor you will still have to see off any other rivals for your catch. So you must take it to a place where none of them can reach you. That will be very difficult. But all this will certainly simulate the usual events in the life of a vagabond cat during the hardest part of the year.'

Sammy was stunned, unable to make any reply, let alone protest. His pet's background made him innocent of the truth: that Brute was the sole author of this test imposed on him, and that it was nothing to do with the coming of winter. Pinkie, of course, knew better, but she kept silent. She savoured the prospect of Sammy's triumph, and she had no doubt that Brute's cunning would rebound on him. For she had no knowledge of Brute's real motive: to frighten Sammy right away from the area by setting him an impossible task, driving him back to the old easy life under human care.

At last Sammy found his voice. 'You ask a lot of me,' he said.

'Yes,' said Brute. 'We need to.'

'When am I expected to start?'

'Best to get it over with. You could use the rest of the day to prepare yourself.'

Sammy looked at Pinkie, then back at Brute. He wanted Pinkie for his mate. So did Brute. Sammy knew he had not a chance of keeping her if he should let this test defeat him. Pinkie's eyes were telling him so. He had to win her. He turned away, wanting to be alone. Brindle was waiting nearby, but Sammy ignored him.

'That's the last we shall see of Sammy,' Brute muttered to Pinkie. He was confident he had done what Stella had asked of him.

'He won't give up so easily', Pinkie replied. 'You're overlooking something. Like father, like son. Isn't that right, Beau?'

Sammy's Choice

Sammy found some growths of weed where the foliage was still thick and hid himself away. He thought long and hard about what he had to do. A voice inside his head seemed to urge him to abandon his new life with all its difficulties and hardship; he was not made for it. But he fought down this impulse. He had thrown in his lot with the vagabond cats and must abide by the commitment. His newly won reputation was at stake. The most important thing to do now, he decided, was to eat well, before his ordeal commenced. This would give him a flying start. He went first in search of mice.

Since this was his last opportunity to hunt for some time, he exercised all his considerable patience and new-found skill. Eventually he had collected together four bank voles and a fieldmouse. He ate the fieldmouse and removed the voles to the place where he had done his thinking. He carefully hid these from sight. Then he turned fishing-cat.

On his way to the stream he saw Brownie and Mottle. They knew where he was going but did not attempt to accompany him. At the waterside Sammy was less lucky. It began to rain and the disturbed water made it impossible for him to see the fish. However, he did manage to hook one out early on. It was a minnow and he ate it immediately. As the rain fell more heavily he gave up the fishing expedition and took up shelter under the nearby trees. Quite unexpectedly, his luck turned good again.

A wood-pigeon came to sip from a puddle at the edge of the tree-line, only a short distance from where Sammy sheltered. The cat was half-sitting, half-lying, his back pressed against the trunk of a holly tree. The pigeon had its back to him; its head bent to the puddle. It was a large, plump bird. Sammy had never tried to catch one before, but this was easy. He dashed out on his silent paws and pounced on the bird, killing it before it had time to struggle. Muddy water splashed all over Sammy but he took no notice. The pigeon did not make a sound, but many others of its kind went clattering through the branches in alarm, sending smaller birds darting amongst the tree-tops.

Sammy picked up his kill and looked for a place of concealment under the trees. He knew it was no good taking it back to the bomb site. The bird was too big to escape the notice of the other cats. But the ground here was too bare to hide anything. Grasping the pigeon firmly in his clenched jaws, Sammy climbed a little way up the holly tree and wedged this future meal in a joint between branch and trunk. As he descended again he thought of his first hesitant climbing of the apple tree in Mrs Lambert's garden. How long ago that seemed. And how far away!

Now he lost no time in retracing his journey. The afternoon was well on and the allotment beckoned. Sammy was used to ignoring the wet weather. He cared nothing for wet fur. Vagabond cats had not the leisure nor the means to keep themselves dry. He was well ahead of the others and hoped the rain would not keep the rabbits at home. They did not always choose to feed where they knew danger lurked, wet weather or not.

When dusk began to steal over the landscape, Sammy

had been lying in wait for an hour or two. It rained inter-
mittently. Sunny and Patch had spotted Sammy and he
had seen them. None of the others appeared to be
around. Darkness fell softly. Soon Sammy knew there
were to be no rabbits that evening. But he still waited. He
guessed Sunny and Patch had left. Presently there was a
movement close by. Sammy turned his head. The dark
body of the limping Scruff was approaching.

'You're wasting your time,' Scruff informed him.

'There are other animals apart from rabbits that come
here,' Sammy told him.

'Are there? What are they?' Scruff sounded eager.

'I'm not sure. I only hear them. Too dark to see. But if
one should stray too close. . . .'

'Hardly worth hanging around,' Scruff said grumpily.
'If they're hedgehogs we couldn't deal with them
anyway.'

'Why are you here, then?'

'You know I always come searching for scraps.'

'You won't find any tonight.'

'No. Won't be the first time though. And I hear you'll
be doing the same thing from now on.'

'*What* have you heard?' Sammy queried.

'Brute's told us all of your survival test,' Scruff
explained. 'You haven't a chance.'

'You've made out all right,' Sammy countered. 'Scraps
keep you alive.'

'Up till now. I can catch mice too,' Scruff growled. 'But
what hope have I got if you're competing with me?'

'That's your problem,' Sammy responded unhelpfully.

'I don't mean to starve. And what about the winter?'

'What d'you mean?' Scruff sounded more sullen
than usual.

'According to Brute, carrion is the best any of us can
hope for in the cold period.'

'That depends. You have to take your opportunities as they come along. Sometimes you can beg a bit from humans.'

'What? You go up to the houses?'

'It's been known,' Scruff answered shortly. 'I've never done very well at it. I usually get driven away. I suppose they don't like my looks.'

Sammy felt a twinge of sympathy despite himself. 'Well, look, Scruff,' he said, 'this test of mine doesn't last for ever. Don't be too despondent. I want you to survive too.'

'You're a strange animal,' Scruff declared. 'You seem to have two minds. What is it to you whether I survive or not? More food all round if I don't.'

Sammy thought about that. He did not know himself why he cared one way or the other. Perhaps it was just that he did not want to feel he would be to blame for another's death. 'We'll make out,' he murmured. 'Both of us.'

Scruff lapsed into silence. After a while Sammy no longer knew if he was around or not. He himself waited on. There was nothing else to do. He was hungry and he thought of the voles and the pigeon. He resisted the temptation to return to them. He did not know how long they might have to last him.

As the night drew on, however, he heard nothing more than the cry of an owl. He left the allotment and returned to his cache of voles. He ate one and then went on the prowl, hoping to disturb more small creatures to add to his stock. By morning he had collected together a couple of shrews and another fieldmouse.

Sammy looked at his little food dump. These tiny animals represented no more than two modest meals for him. The thought of the plump pigeon, safely stowed away elsewhere, was rather comforting to him. The rain had ceased and he fell into a doze.

Brute was making a search of the waste ground and old allotments. He wanted to ascertain that Sammy had departed as he had predicted. Pinkie stepped daintily behind him, but kept well to the rear. She was equally interested. As they covered more and more ground and found no trace of him, Pinkie became increasingly despondent. Sammy had let her down. Brute, on the other hand, was jubilant.

'Sammy's got sense,' he called behind him. 'He's back where he belongs.'

'He belongs here,' Pinkie muttered beneath her breath. 'And to me. Oh Sammy. . . .'

The object of their search awoke, sure that he could hear Pinkie's voice. He edged out of his hiding place warily. He did not want those mice to be noticed. Then he sat down in full view of any of the vagabonds who cared to look. Pinkie cared very much. She gave a mew of pleasure and ran up to him.

'I knew you wouldn't go!' she exulted and rubbed herself affectionately against him, nuzzling him and seeming perfectly heedless that Brute was watching.

Sammy's father was angry at the display but tried not to show it. He stalked forward very stiffly and growled, 'You're on your own from now on, Sammy. I'll be keeping a constant look-out for you. You know the rules. No hunting. The other cats will report to me if they see the rules broken. It'll be quite a while before you pull down a rabbit again, or even pounce on a mouse. I alone will decide when.' Brute went on his way with the same stiff and purposeful gait.

'Aren't you going to wish me luck?' Sammy cried to him cheekily. This was for Pinkie's benefit. She was purring loudly.

Brute did not answer but he had heard all right. He

really was torn between anger and pride in his son. He disappeared, but Pinkie and Sammy were soon joined by Sunny.

'Don't try any cleverness,' the ginger said unpleasantly. 'If Brute isn't watching you all the time, I shall be. I want to see you so hungry you'll eat dirt.'

'You're a spiteful creature, aren't you?' Sammy returned. 'No, I shan't play any tricks, since you're so concerned. But I may just have a surprise or two in store for you. I don't intend to be beaten, nor humbled, for your amusement.'

'Sunny's jealous of you,' Pinkie said to Sammy. Then she said to the ginger cat, 'Sammy will survive to supersede you, never fear. Scruff has lived off scraps for years and here's Sammy with four good legs.'

'Accidents sometimes happen,' the ginger cat sneered. He turned abruptly and left them, his fur in a bristle.

Sammy was not in the least perturbed by the veiled threat. He was strong, fast and resilient. And he had an admirer in Pinkie who made him more eager than ever to prove himself.

'Listen, Sammy,' Pinkie said in a low voice, now they were alone. 'I'm going to help you. My appetite's not very great. I can eat less. I can still hunt and what I don't eat—'

'You're very generous, Pinkie,' Sammy said warmly. 'But I'd rather do this on my own. I'll find food because I'll have to. And when I do hunt again the next rabbit I catch will be the biggest you've ever seen. You and I will feast together on it as a celebration. I have a feeling Brute's day is coming to an end. So I'm willing to be tried and tested. I'll be the stronger for it, and more resourceful than ever.'

'Brave cat,' Pinkie whispered. Sammy's response to her suggestion was all she could have wished. She knew in her bones the time was not far off when Brute and Sammy would meet in that first – and last – great clash. And Sammy's youth was on his side.

'My rest was interrupted,' Sammy said next. 'I must sleep for long stretches now and save energy. You'd better return to Brute, at least for the present. We'll see each other soon and—' He broke off.

'And what?' Pinkie prompted.

'You look after yourself too.'

'Of course I will. I'm a vagabond, am I not?'

—15—

The Test Begins

Sammy's period in Quartermile Field had sharpened his wits and he had some ideas of his own of how to exploit his opportunities, whilst still sticking to the conditions Brute had laid down. He was allowed carrion only – so be it. Carrion was any dead animal so, although he himself could not hunt, there was nothing to stop him dispossessing another cat of prey *it* had killed. With this plan of action in his head, Sammy fell asleep near his store of mice and voles.

However, aside from Pinkie, he had other friends amongst the vagabonds. There was Brindle, who certainly meant to be of assistance whenever he could. Brindle had decided that any carrion or scraps he came across must be reserved for Sammy, whereas in the past they would simply have been left for Scruff. He would tell Sammy of anything he found, and his sister Brownie was prepared to do the same. Then there was Patch, who had some sympathy with Sammy's predicament. The old cat knew very well the test set him was preposterous and designed to defeat him. Patch had been impressed before by Sammy's readiness to adapt to a life that was quite foreign to him. Now, without actually being able to provide him with food, he would make sure that anything he caught could be won by Sammy, if the young tabby was determined enough. For Patch alone had guessed what Sammy's tactics would be.

Lastly, and strangest of all, there was Brute himself. Envious he might be, but the King Cat had been surprised at Sammy taking up his challenge. He had not desired this and it had not been his design. Now he could see there was more to Sammy than he had recognized at first. He admired his courage and, as his father, how could he allow him to suffer more than was compatible with the vagabonds' own sufferings? None of the other cats had been required to pass such a test of endurance. He thought about Stella. Whatever would she think of him if she knew about this? She had asked him to restore Sammy to his comforts, not torment him. So, all in all, Sammy was justified in sleeping peacefully.

When he awoke, the clear autumn light was losing its strength. He ate one of his mice and took stock of his situation. There was no need to move yet. He did not feel hungry. He watched the light fade gradually. He blinked in the glare of the setting sun, as it dipped behind a row of houses. Suddenly he found himself thinking of Molly. When this ordeal was behind him, Sammy decided, he would go back and tell the old dog, his friend, all about it.

In the gathering darkness he tried to imagine what the other cats would be doing. The allotments would be beckoning most of them; the hungry ones anyway. For him they were out of bounds now, except as a thief. And thief he would become. But not yet. He must not strike too early and put them all on their guard. He could afford to wait whilst he still had food. He shivered as a gust of wind whipped through his fur. The dark hours were becoming colder. Sammy needed that shelter. He was certainly not inured to the cold in the way that the other cats were who had been born in the open air. So winter could defeat him even if he should survive this test.

He stirred himself. He wanted to be on the move now for warmth's sake. He threaded his way through the weedy growths, which were dying back with the onset of autumn. Mottle the tortoiseshell scuttled in front of him in the blackness and ran on without a word. He saw Brownie lapping from a pool of rainwater. She kept her eyes on Sammy as she drank. He felt he had suddenly become an outsider again; an object of curiosity.

He left Quartermile Field and wandered morosely in the direction of the stream. When he got to it he wondered why he had come, for fishing was forbidden him. He trotted along to the wood and singled out the holly tree where he had hidden the pigeon. A quick climb and he was assured it was still there and, as yet, remaining fresh. Sammy scrambled down and went pattering over the first fallen leaves under the trees. He had never explored the entire wood. Now seemed a good time to do so.

The trees rustled and shook in the strong breeze, drowning out other noises. Sammy knew nothing of the habits of nocturnal wild animals, so he had no fear. Half-heartedly he chased a few dry leaves about as they spun in the wind. He came across a hedgehog making a meal of a slug and smacking its lips over it with the greatest enjoyment. Sammy wondered what a slug would taste like. The hedgehog ran away at his approach.

After a while the young tabby tired of the deep darkness of the wood. He ambled unhurriedly towards its perimeter, startling a small animal which raced across his path. Sammy gave chase. The creature easily eluded him and was soon safe in its hole. He left the wood and made his way to the houses where the cats sometimes begged food in the winter. These were unfamiliar buildings to Sammy, but he soon found that they looked very like those near his old mistress. He was quite at home in gardens and went from one to another, investigating everything. Lights shone out from windows but the gardens were empty of life. No chickens here, no dogs and no cats. All safely shut up, he supposed.

A door opened in one house, briefly throwing out a patch of light into the adjoining garden. Sammy heard human voices again for the first time since he had heard his mistress calling him. There was the rattle of a dustbin and then the door closed again. Sammy sat down and meditated. The voices, friendly and cheerful, took him back to his time as a kitten. How he had loved his mistress's voice: sometimes shrill, sometimes soft, but always so kindly. He even recalled the gardening boy, Edward. Did he miss contact with humans? He thought he must do, otherwise why was he thinking about them now? Supposing he had never heard about Beau and his kind of life, would he have been content to stay where he had been born and brought up? No, no. That was not possible. His father's influence would still have worked on him. Stella's authority had waned as he got older, just as his father's invisible sway had grown. And where *was* Beau? Would he ever meet him? It was strange they had not encountered each other somewhere. Sammy could not help thinking that, if they should do so some time in the future, he would feel himself to be on a par with his father. He was no longer the naïve domestic pet.

'Didn't expect to find you up here so soon,' a voice behind him spoke abruptly.

Sammy jumped. Lost in his thoughts about Beau, it was as if he had caused his father suddenly to materialize in the darkness. But it was only Scruff.

'I – er – was just exploring a bit,' Sammy replied.

'Found anything?'

'No. I wasn't actually looking for food.'

'Get away.'

'No, I've got a small amount put by for a day or two.'

'Have you? And here I've come,' Scruff said, 'because I thought you'd beat me to all the scraps on our patch.'

'We haven't come to that just yet,' said Sammy. 'I'll leave the coast clear for you for the present. It's turning colder, isn't it?'

'Don't talk about it. But this is nothing. You wait till the frost starts to nip at you. Oh, it's difficult to keep still at night.'

'Do you find yourself any cover in the winter?'

'There isn't much to be had,' Scruff answered grimly. 'Paper's a good thing if you can find any. It gets blown into the area sometimes. There's always a fight for it. You can guess how I fare. Best I can hope for is to climb in amongst the brambles.'

'Have you always been lame?' Sammy asked.

'Pretty well. Wasn't born like it though. I got into a fight, of course; got bitten very badly. Never been the same since.'

'What happened to the other cat?'

'Cat? It was a dog.'

'A dog!'

'Yes. Don't sound so surprised. Dogs are no friends to us. They chase us and – well, I got caught. But I gave it something to remember. You should have heard it yelp!'

'Dogs aren't always like that,' Sammy said slowly, thinking naturally of Molly.

'Aren't they? Don't you believe it!' Scruff rasped.

Sammy could not but be reminded of their different backgrounds.

'Then there's the stone-throwing I told you about,' Scruff went on. 'That really finished my leg good and proper.'

'Yes,' said Sammy. 'I can see that. Well, I won't interrupt you. You'll prefer to be alone, no doubt.'

'Wouldn't say that,' Scruff muttered in his gruff way. 'You're not like the others. They haven't much time for me.'

'Just as you like then,' Sammy said brightly. He was glad Scruff had appeared.

'Shall we see if we can rustle something up?' the lame black cat offered.

'All right.'

'I haven't eaten well for days,' he went on. 'I could do with something tasty. Your human friends are very wasteful. You can sometimes dig a bit of their food out for yourself without needing to beg for it.'

'Well – lead on then,' Sammy said. Here was a new experience in store.

Scruff went unevenly across the garden, sniffing carefully. He had an acute sense of smell, and relied on his nose to lead him to food. It was his best asset.

'I don't think there's anything around here,' he said. 'Let's try the next one.'

They got into the neighbouring garden. Sammy was surprised to see that Scruff managed to climb well enough, despite his game leg.

'Much more promising,' was the black cat's verdict. His nose was inhaling with gusto. 'There's something about.'

Sammy followed him. Scruff found some discarded rib-bones left over from a barbecue. For the life of him Sammy could not see that they could be eaten. But Scruff did not hesitate. He grabbed one greedily and began to gnaw. Sammy watched him.

As Scruff moved on to the next one he said, 'There's enough for you.'

'Yes,' said Sammy, 'but surely—'

'Oh, you can get something off 'em,' Scruff told him. 'Can't pick and choose, can we?'

'No, I suppose not,' said Sammy. He took one of the ribs, more because he did not want to seem to be turning up his nose at it than because he thought it would do him any good. He was not at all used to bones and had no idea how to treat them. Scruff, of course, was an old hand. He knew just how to pin a bone down at one end so as to be able to lick or gnaw at the scraps of meat still attached. Sammy would have done well to have tried to ape him – that would have been the safest method. But, instead, he stupidly attempted to chew the bone itself, crunching it up and splintering it into sharp fragments.

It was only a matter of time before one of these dangerous shards of bone fixed itself in his throat. Sammy began to cough in a cat's typically wheezy fashion. The more he coughed the more the bone seemed to penetrate. His coughs became more violent. He began to choke.

'Spit it out! Spit it out!' Scruff called to him urgently.

But Sammy could do nothing to help himself. He gasped and wheezed, his sides heaved, he lowered his head to the ground. His whole body was racked by the spasms of the painful choking coughs. He could not draw breath, his eyes began to dim. . . .

'Jump about a bit, shake your head,' Scruff advised. 'You might loosen it.'

Sammy could no longer hear him. The bone was lodged fast and his strength seemed to be ebbing away. Still he coughed, savagely, painfully, as if his throat was being torn across. A final gurgling choke came from his mouth, his legs shook and then collapsed under him. He sank to his belly; his chin rested on the ground. There was a horrible stillness.

Scruff limped to his side, expecting the worst. But there was life still in Sammy's eyes. They gazed at the lame cat with a hopeless expression. The splinter of bone had shifted its position slightly but only sufficient to allow the young tabby to take shallow breaths of air. He dared not move for fear of it choking him again. He could not speak. He lay almost motionless.

'You should never try to swallow bone,' Scruff said unhelpfully. 'I didn't realize; I would have told you before. Lie still now until you feel easier. Perhaps you've dislodged it. If not, there's nothing to be done.'

Even in his agony Sammy was struck by the apparent heartlessness of Scruff's remarks. But he knew that the vagabond cats' (and, in particular, Scruff's) attitude to life was one of resignation. The hardship and perils they constantly faced made life a tenuous sort of thing. It was a never-ending struggle and when they themselves could no longer cope with it, then they accepted their lot unquestioningly.

Sammy's breath gradually came a little more easily. Still he dared not stir. Scruff was disinclined to stay with him. He was restless. He would limp away from Sammy a little way and then come back to examine him again.

The lame black cat needed to spend a good deal of his time in scavenging. It was the only way he could get enough to eat. So far this night he had found almost nothing. Sammy did not want him to stay around. Scruff could not assist him. He tried to indicate this in his expression but Scruff could not quite bring himself to desert Sammy. And so he would wander to and fro while, at the same time, wishing he were elsewhere.

At last Sammy could bear this no longer. He struggled slowly to his feet, keeping his head hanging low so as not

to set off the coughing again. His breathing was much
freer now and he felt himself recovering.

'You – need – not linger – here,' he managed to gasp.
'I'll – manage.' He could feel the sharpness of the bone in
his gullet as he panted out the words but, thankfully, he
did not dislodge it again. He knew it was too big a piece
for him to swallow right down. If only it did not move
from its present position he would at least be able to
breathe. He longed to take a drink. Perhaps there was a
pool of water lying somewhere in the garden. There had
been a lot of rain. He would have to move very, very
slowly to look.

Scruff muttered something which Sammy did not
catch and left him. Sammy began to haul himself along,
one pace at a time, keeping his body low and his head
perfectly still. He spied a place where rain water had
collected against a wall of the house and edged himself
towards it. His throat was sore and burning. He stared at
the water. How cool and refreshing it looked. But he was
scared. He did not know what would happen if he should
try to swallow again. However, he had no option but to
try. He must drink. He lapped a little and, very gently, he
swallowed. The water slid down quite easily. He could
feel the bone fragment as he drank but it stayed where it
had come to rest.

Sammy was encouraged and perked up a bit. He
finished his drink and wondered what to do next. He
could not remain in this strange garden. Now his breathing was a little better, and he could move more easily. He
decided to return to the waste ground. There was no
choice for him.

He moved across the garden carefully, but with more
like his usual gait. Now came his biggest problem. The
fence. How could he jump and climb with a lump of
bone in his gullet? But he remembered Scruff's advice

when he had first started choking. He had recommended jumping as a means of loosening the object. Sammy sprang at the fence and pulled himself up. Nothing happened. There was only the constant nagging consciousness of the bone digging into his throat. It was firmly fixed.

Slowly he made his way to his hideaway in the undergrowth. Brindle saw him before he got there. He noticed something awkward about Sammy's movements, and came towards him.

'Anything wrong?' he asked.

'Yes. How do you know?' Sammy wheezed.

'Well, you seem to be sort of – slinking,' said Brindle.

'I'm in pain.'

'What is it?'

'A piece of bone – stuck in my throat.'

Brindle was aware that this usually meant death for a cat in the wild. He did not know what to say. But Sammy knew very well what straits he was in.

'You needn't look like that,' he gasped. 'I suppose the game's up with me.'

'How did it happen?'

'Does it matter? It happened. I can't – talk well.'

'I'm sorry, Sammy. Can I help you at all?'

'How?'

'I – don't know.'

'You can't, Brindle. You would if you could. I know.'

'If you try eating, the food might carry the bone down,' Brindle suggested.

'I don't think so. It's too big. Don't – concern yourself. I just want to rest.'

Sammy pushed his way through the weeds and slumped down. He was weary and frightened. His remaining stock of mice stared him in the face. He began to consider what Brindle had said. Fright had taken away his appetite, but he knew it would eventually return with a vengeance. And supposing Brindle had been right? The more he looked at the mice, the more Sammy was tempted to take the gamble. After all, he could not stay as he was indefinitely. He lay a bit longer and then suddenly, in a mood of do or die, he snatched up one of the mice and began to eat.

No sooner did the first mouthful of food reach his throat than he began to choke all over again. This time his coughs were even more violent and more painful than before. The mouthful would not pass the obstruction. Sammy coughed it out but the bone dug deeper still. The coughs gradually subsided as before, but now Sammy knew the worst. He could no longer eat. If the bone stayed in his throat he would die of starvation.

16

Survival of the Fittest

The days passed slowly for Sammy. The splinter of bone did not seem to shift. He shunned company, trying to sleep as much as possible in his usual place. It was the one way he could forget the pain and discomfort. He moved only occasionally to take a few laps of water. He grew thin and weak. Scruff and Brindle knew of Sammy's misery but they could do nothing to help him. Brute was sure he had given up and gone back to Stella. Pinkie, however, silently kept faith with Sammy. She believed he would reappear eventually.

The only other cat who had any real interest in the tabby's whereabouts was Sunny, who had been keeping his eyes open for Sammy all along. Sunny was sure the young cat would try to evade Brute's demands somehow, and he meant to stop him. He made regular tours of the area in search of Sammy and at last one day he happened to come upon him as he drank. The ginger cat noticed at once Sammy's listless appearance. He had never forgotten how he had lost the fight with Sammy over the rabbit, and now he saw his chance to turn the tables on him. Sammy was clearly at a disadvantage.

Sammy noticed the ginger cat's reflection in the puddle where he was drinking. He looked up and saw Sunny watching him, ginger tail swishing ominously. Sammy knew he was intent on trouble, and he was afraid. He could expect no sympathy from this animal for his present plight. He must avoid a fight if he could or it might be the end of him. The cats stared at each other. Sammy was ready to run.

'You've lost weight,' Sunny observed. 'We're more of an even match now.'

Sammy knew it was pointless to remonstrate and in any case he was not given time. The ginger leapt at him. Sammy darted away. But his legs seemed unwilling to carry him. They had lost their speed. He tried to shake off his pursuer by running through the vegetation, then quickly changing his direction, but he knew he had no choice of avoiding him for long. Sunny caught him up and was upon him. They went bowling down a bank, locked together, and Sammy landed with the other cat on top of him. He was pressed hard against the ground. He began to gasp under the weight and, as he gasped, the awful coughing returned. Sunny released him and stood away. He seemed to think he had done enough to avenge himself.

Sammy went on coughing, and now he thought he would never catch his breath again. Each cough shook his whole body: he felt he would cough up his life in a few more moments. There was a tearing sensation in his throat and Sammy shuddered under the most violent cough of all. Then something entered his mouth from low down in his throat and he spat it on to the ground in front of him.

It was the fragment of bone.

The coughing fit subsided and, weak as a new-born kitten, Sammy stared at the tiny object that had nearly killed him. He swallowed hard several times. His throat was on fire. It burnt mercilessly. But there was no block-age there any longer.

Sunny had disappeared by now, alarmed despite himself at the spectacle Sammy had presented. The tabby stayed still for a while longer, enjoying the sense of relief, and breathing in deep breaths. It was then that Brindle found him.

'Oh Sammy,' he said gravely, 'you look terrible.'

'Ah but, Brindle,' Sammy croaked, 'I feel marvellous.'

'I don't understand you.'

'Come here. Look.' Sammy showed him the piece of bone. 'Now I'm free again.'

Brindle was delighted. 'I really thought it was all up with you,' he said.

'Oh no,' Sammy replied in a whisper. 'Not yet.'

'Brownie and I – we saved some scraps for you,' Brindle said excitedly. 'We were going to eat them, but now—'

'Take me to them,' Sammy croaked, 'though first I must drink again. My throat feels like an open wound.'

Brindle's scraps proved worthless. Brownie had eaten most of them and now only a few odd dried-up pieces were left.

'Leave them for Scruff,' Sammy remarked. 'I've got a better store myself.'

'Sorry, Sammy,' Brindle said contritely.

'Forget it. I'll look after myself.' Sammy returned with haste to his stock of mice. He ate two. They tasted vile but he did not care. All he was concerned about was that he could swallow once again. Already his throat had eased a bit, and his hunger was returning in a healthy sort of way. Now he had to regain his strength for the real test ahead. In late afternoon he set off to fetch his pigeon.

Of course the holly tree had long ago been stripped of this source of food. It was not in the nature of keen-eyed crows and magpies to overlook such a bounty. But Sammy was dismayed. He had really been counting on this food to build himself up. Well, there was no help for it. He must now put his other plan into effect.

At dusk he hid himself well to the rear of the several vagabonds who lay hopefully waiting for the rabbits' arrival. Brute was there and so was Sunny, but Sammy wanted nothing to do with them. He was hoping that Patch or Mottle or even Pinkie would be lucky in the hunt. Weak as he was, he felt he had an even chance against any of these. All the cats waited eagerly. Soon their patience was rewarded: three rabbits, all youngsters, came searching out their favourite food-plants without much caution. As soon as the time was right, Brute made sure of one of them.

Most of the cats had aimed for the same rabbit and so fell back obediently as the King Cat rushed out. The second rabbit escaped. The third bolted in the direction of Patch. Patch was no longer swift but he had a lifetime of experience in rabbit-hunting. He did not betray his presence until the last possible moment. The rabbit was crushed and held firm before it knew much about it. Sammy watched avidly. He wanted to be positive that the animal was dead.

Patch grabbed his prey by the neck, preparing to carry it away. Since he had lost several of his teeth he found it difficult to get a good grip on large animals, so he had to drop the rabbit frequently and begin again. Sammy soon noted this. It was just the opportunity he had hoped for. It was obvious the rabbit was lifeless. There was not the slightest movement about it as Patch dropped it, hauled it a little way, then dropped it again. It was carrion.

Sammy did not intend to fight for it. He did not think Patch would fight him anyway. He merely walked over and, when old Patch had to let his quarry go once more, Sammy commandeered it and made off without a word.

Patch was completely taken aback. He had not seen Sammy in days – had almost forgotten his existence.

Now here he was, appearing from nowhere, and snatching his dinner off him. Patch made no attempt to give chase. He just sat down with a bemused expression on his face. The sheer cheek of it! It was outrageous that Sammy should get away with it – but he was going to let him. Sammy deserved it. He certainly looked as if he needed the food more than Patch felt he did himself.

Naturally the other cats had seen what had happened. They reacted in different ways.

'Get after him, Patch!' snarled Sunny. 'The thief!'

Pinkie was overjoyed to see Sammy again but shocked by his appearance. She ran past Patch who still sat staring, and caught up the young tabby.

'How clever of you, Sammy,' she chattered. 'I've missed you. I thought you'd forgotten me.'

Sammy's one interest for the present was food. That was the only reason he had shown himself. As his jaws were fully employed with his load, he merely grunted and moved on his way. Pinkie fell back, disappointed. Her eyes, however, told her that Sammy must nearly have starved, and she understood his preoccupation.

Brute was watching with mixed feelings. He was, first of all, surprised that Sammy was still around. He regretted that he had failed to drive him away from the area. As Pinkie ran eagerly after his son, a wave of jealousy swept over him – he was reminded once again that he had a rival. But Sammy's coolness in dispossessing Patch earned Brute's grudging admiration. It seemed that he meant to prove that he was by no means beaten, despite his sufferings. Brute took a decision. It was obvious Sammy had experienced great difficulty finding food. Yet he had not given up. There was one final chance of fulfilling Stella's wishes and also of ridding himself of Sammy's rivalry. That was to demand that now his son must deal with the next part of the test.

Leaving his own kill where it lay, Brute followed Sammy's direction. He did not intend to speak now, but he wanted to know where Sammy could be located. The young tabby had dragged Patch's rabbit through the gap in the high wire fence and was on his way to his own corner of the vegetation. Brute kept him in view.

Sunny was furious that Sammy appeared to be getting away. Patch had not moved at all and Brute, the King Cat himself, was clearly not going to do anything.

'This can't be borne!' he snarled to Pinkie, who happened to be nearest to him. 'What's wrong with you all? Can't you see what that animal's up to?'

'Why are you so interested, Sunny?' Pinkie asked sweetly. 'It's not your rabbit.'

'No, and it's not Sammy's either!' the ginger cat cried. 'Just let him try that with me.'

'What a state you're getting yourself in,' Mottle remarked.

At last Patch spoke up. 'Save your anger for your own affairs,' he said. 'If I'm not bothered, why should you be?'

'But . . . but . . . how can you just—' spluttered Sunny.

'Just allow it?' Patch suggested. 'Oh, I suppose because of a sneaking respect for Sammy. And a certain amount of sympathy.'

'Sympathy! That beats everything! Of all the stupid—'

'Oh, do shut up, Sunny,' said Pinkie. 'Your envy is very tedious.'

'Envy?' growled Sunny. 'Of a human's pet?'

'He doesn't look much like a pet any more,' Patch answered him.

'That's what he can't stand,' Pinkie observed. 'That Sammy is as much a vagabond now as he is.'

Brute saw Sammy to his hideout and turned away. He

was not going to interrupt his meal for a while. He returned for his own catch.

'It's time for the next phase of the trial,' he announced to the others.

The other cats knew perfectly well what that entailed. Sammy was to be allowed to hunt for himself again now that he looked too weak to be able to manage it.

'I still think Sammy will fool us all,' Pinkie said confidently.

'He's fooled me very well already,' Patch remarked ruefully.

'He won't fool me,' Sunny vowed. 'I'll see to it that he never catches another rabbit.'

The other cats ignored him. They thought his obsession was ludicrous. Even Brute's face held an expression of contempt.

That night the King Cat sought out his son. Sammy had eaten his first good meal for days and was feeling quite cheerful. He greeted Brute with the remark, 'I suppose you've come to reprimand me?'

'No,' answered his father. 'Why should I? No, I've come for quite another reason. It seems to me that recently you must have got quite a good idea of what life in the winter can be like?'

'I've had some difficulties,' Sammy acknowledged. He did not enlarge on them.

'I can see that you have. So now it's time for you to prove that, despite them, you can still look after yourself. And I mean – by showing you've retained the strength to hunt.'

Sammy's ears pricked up. 'Ah, now I can resume hunting? I wondered when you'd say the word. But look at me. Just what d'you think I'm capable of hunting now?'

'I don't know,' said Brute. 'But the only true test is a

rabbit, and that's what you'll have to deal with. You remember the rules.'

'The way I feel I should think the rabbit will be in a fitter state to deal with *me*.'

'That's your problem,' Brute said, shortly. 'Tomorrow at dusk I'll be watching for you.' He left abruptly. He did not doubt that Sammy would fall at the next hurdle. Stella would have Sammy restored to her soon afterwards.

The next day Sammy ate another portion of rabbit. His throat troubled him much less now and, altogether, he began to feel stronger. At dusk he encountered Brute by the vagabonds' entrance to the allotment area. Without a word the King Cat led Sammy through. It was still sufficiently light for Sammy to see that all the cats were present, even Scruff. They all appeared to be waiting for his arrival. Sunny was pacing to and fro in a nervous sort of way.

'Choose your position, Sammy,' Brute said.

Sammy looked around uncertainly. 'The rabbits don't always come,' he muttered. 'What if we don't see any?'

'You'll just have to trust to your luck,' was the answer.

The other cats were silent. But Brindle watched Sammy settle himself and then joined him. 'I think Sunny is up to something,' he whispered.

Certainly the ginger was the only animal still on his feet. Suddenly Sammy recalled that, even if he should catch a rabbit, he must then fight one of the other cats (whom Brute would select) for its possession. So Sunny must be the candidate – his nervousness betrayed him. Sammy was not optimistic. In his present state, he could not hope to do very well against Sunny, the second most powerful animal amongst the vagabonds.

'He's going to fight me,' he answered Brindle.

Sammy's friend made no comment. He did not have to. It was obvious what he was thinking.

However, Brute had not chosen Sunny, nor any other cat, to fight his son. In his mind there was no need, since Sammy's hunting was not going to be successful. In fact Sunny's restlessness was part of a plan known only to himself. He stayed on his feet so that he would be the first of the cats to know if rabbits were coming to feed. He had no intention of allowing Sammy the remotest chance.

There was a long wait in store for the vagabonds. They began to get irritated with Sunny's continual pacing. They were there on their own account, as well as to witness Sammy's performance.

'How do you expect rabbits to venture here when they can see you moving about?' Patch demanded of the ginger.

'Why should you worry?' Sunny snapped at him. 'You can't keep the ones you catch anyway.'

'Lie down, Sunny! What are you doing this for?' Mottle and Brownie called out together.

Pinkie guessed it was some plan to thwart Sammy, and added her voice. 'You're spoiling all our chances,' she cried, 'including your own!'

Sunny glared at her but, in the end, with all the cats objecting, he was obliged to submit.

For a long time there was no sound. But at last a faint rustling roused their hopes. Sunny jumped up again. There was a solitary, elderly-looking rabbit moving unsteadily through the plants, nibbling here and there. It looked so slow and feeble that it seemed to Sunny that even Scruff could manage it. To forestall Sammy he raced out at the old creature, not with the idea of catching it, but simply to scare it off. The rabbit was busy chewing a cabbage leaf and did not see its danger at once. But, when

Sunny was almost on it and could have pounced, it turned tail and loped away. It had no great speed and was, quite obviously, badly hampered by age.

The other cats had held back, naturally assuming they had no hope with Sunny so far in advance. But when he showed no signs of wishing to bring the animal down, they spurted belatedly into action, Sammy amongst them.

From a prone start, Sammy had the advantage of all of them. He quickly left them behind and gained on his elderly quarry and its initial pursuer. Sunny looked round and saw the tabby drawing close. He ran across his path, meaning to check him.

Sammy instinctively leapt upwards. He cleared Sunny's body at a bound and, in the next few strides, drew level with the rabbit and pulled it down. A younger animal would have escaped him, but this one had neither the swiftness nor the strength necessary. Sammy killed his victim and began to drag it back towards Brute as proof of his success.

But Sunny was not finished yet. He was furious, both with Sammy and with himself. With a howl he launched himself at the tabby. Sammy dropped the rabbit in order to defend himself. His run had left him feeling quite shaky. He was no longer a match for the big ginger and could only try to save himself from injury.

Sunny's weight pinned Sammy to the ground. For the second time the tabby was at the ginger's mercy, but he was not entirely without strength and he struggled to free himself.

'The rabbit's . . . yours . . . if you want it,' Sammy panted.

'I don't want it,' Sunny snapped.

'Then why—' Sammy broke off as he saw the other cats clustering around to watch the contest. His eyes met

Pinkie's. She was soundlessly pleading for Sammy's release in her heart, but her eyes put a new spirit into Sammy. He was suddenly reminded of what he would lose if he should give up now.

He exerted an extra burst of strength, shook Sunny clear and grabbed the rabbit again. Without a backward glance he moved off as quickly as he could towards the high wire fence. The rabbit bumped over the ground between Sammy's forelegs. The cat's jaws and his shoulders ached unbearably. Sunny lost time as he gaped at the retreating animal in astonishment. He had been pitched on his back, much to his surprise, and, restored to his feet, hesitated before deciding upon his next action.

Galvanized into action once more, Sunny dashed to the hole in the fence for the final tussle. But he had forgotten Sammy's skill and also the terms of the test of survival. Sammy, however, had not. He was going to see it through to the end.

At the foot of the wire fence Sammy took a firmer grip on the carcass. Then, shakily, and extremely slowly, he edged his way up the swaying fence, just as he had done once before.

The other vagabonds crowded around the base, but none of them attempted to follow. Only Sammy had ever climbed up the wire. Pinkie was in the greatest excitement. Brute stared, willing Sammy to drop his burden, to give up, even to fall . . .

Yet Sammy clung on. He thought he never would – never could – reach the top. Exhaustion was engulfing him, but his will was strong. His eyes swam, his body trembled, yet still he mounted. At last the top was reached. He staggered once or twice, then crawled along the top to a point from where he could look down on them all. The fence wavered and rattled. The rabbit's weight dragged at his jaws. But Sammy was immovable. He knew none of the cats could get to him. The test was over.

Pinkie cried out, 'Sammy! Sammy! Sammy has triumphed!' She turned to Brute. 'I knew it, I knew it,' she chanted. 'I knew he would do it.' She was ecstatic.

Brute looked at her without a word. He felt that his reign was coming to an end. The other cats, too, were silent. All of them knew that Sammy had done more, far more, than any of them had ever done. It had never been necessary, nor expected of them to perform such feats. They were humbled, even stunned. Sunny was the first to slink away. Soon Brute, too, disappeared and, one by one, the others followed. When only Pinkie remained Sammy at last let the rabbit drop. The little white cat ignored it. She mewed to her hero to come down. Slowly Sammy descended.

17

The King Cat

Pinkie stayed with Sammy until he recovered. A drizzle of rain began to fall. Its chill dampness acted like a tonic on the exhausted young tabby. He heard Pinkie's purrs, saw her bright eyes so close to him and knew, beyond any doubt, that he had proved himself.

When Sammy was ready, Pinkie led the way to the broken-down shelter. Instinctively she had sensed that Brute had vacated the area. Sure enough, there was no sign of him. He had gone wandering again.

Later, under the fence, the forgotten rabbit was stealthily carried away by Scruff.

A few days passed and Sammy was once more himself. Pinkie and Brindle brought food, and even Scruff offered the less tasty parts of the elderly rabbit Sammy had caught. But soon Sammy was a hunter again, and then the skills he had acquired really came to the fore. His great speed and a new kind of cunning ensured that he never went hungry and, because of this, neither did Pinkie. The vagabonds realized that the old King Cat had been superseded. The deference they had paid to Brute was now paid, in his absence, to Sammy. Sunny kept himself out of sight as much as he could. He knew that he dare not meddle with a strong, healthy Sammy. He longed for Brute's return. He guessed that eventually there must be a confrontation, for Brute was not likely to cede his supremacy without a battle.

Sammy guessed too. He expected Brute to come back and he knew that, when he did, there could be only one outcome. What he did not know was his special relationship with Brute. And it was that that was keeping the King Cat away.

Brute's attempt to drive Sammy out had failed. Now there was only one course left open to him. But because Sammy was his son, he delayed the inevitable confrontation. He had always known in his bones that one day he and Sammy would have to fight. They were natural rivals – rivals for supremacy, rivals for Pinkie, rivals for the right to be King of Quartermile Field. He did not want to fight Sammy, but his pride prevented him from passively giving ground.

And so one evening Sammy emerged from the hut to find Brute waiting. They looked at each other without a word, each silently calculating the other's strength. Behind Sammy stood Pinkie. She was quaking with anticipation.

At last Brute spoke. 'I think you know why I've come.'

'Yes,' said Sammy. 'I expected you.'

Their tails waved slowly from side to side. They were both very tense. Each waited for the other to make a move. Brute's hesitation was natural. Sammy did not understand the reason for it and suddenly sprang at his father. Brute avoided his lunge and backed away, hissing loudly. Sammy tried again. His claws ripped across Brute's back. Brute returned the blow and now they scratched and bit at close quarters, each trying to pin the other down. Their howls were tremendous. The other vagabonds came running. Sunny's eyes gleamed. He waited for Brute's strength to tell. But Sammy had all the advantages. He was younger, more confident and was unhampered by the knowledge that held Brute back from using his full force. He crushed Brute underneath him, holding him in a vice-like grip. His teeth and claws buried themselves deep in the older cat's flesh. Brute could have thrown him off, but his heart was not in this contest.

'All right, Sammy,' he said. 'I yield.'

For a while Sammy maintained the pressure. He thought Brute might be using a trick. Then he relaxed and the two cats stood looking at each other once more.

'You won't see me again,' Brute said.

Sammy made no answer. The vagabonds looked from father to son as if wondering how their own lives were going to be affected.

Pinkie said, 'Farewell, Beau.'

He looked at her. 'Farewell,' he said.

The name was of no immediate significance to the other cats. But Sammy caught the word and held on to it. Beau! He looked at his rival with new eyes. He saw another tabby: the coat different from his – darker – but tabby nevertheless. His father! Oh, how on earth had he not guessed it! The build, the voice, just as Stella had described them. It had been the name. Brute. Beau. Well, naturally, his father's female admirers would not see him as a brute at all. How much more suitable 'Beau' was for them. And, of course, Brute had known all along whom he was fighting. Now Sammy understood why he had yielded.

'I didn't intend this,' Sammy's father said to him.

'Neither did I,' Sammy whispered. He knew what Brute was thinking. The older cat looked a moment longer, then turned and, with his accustomed dignity, walked away. Sammy had found his father – and lost him again.

The other cats milled about irresolutely. Sunny followed in Brute's wake. There was no place for him any longer in Quartermile Field. The rest could not decide whether to leave or to stay.

Sammy's feelings were complicated. He had been proud of his victory; of becoming the new King Cat with all its advantages. But now it was a hollow pride. How could he be proud of ousting his own father? Should he be the one to leave? To leave the field clear? He stared after his father in the gathering darkness.

For the first time in a long while Sammy thought of Stella. Could she advise him? He had not been good at listening to his mother's advice, but now. . . .

No sooner was the thought there than he decided to go back once more – to Stella and Josephine, to Molly, to his mistress and his birthplace. He left the cluster of cats and set off. It was almost night. He would look for his mother in the old familiar place where he and Josephine had first opened their eyes.

Sammy passed the chicken-run where the cockerel still lorded it over his hens like a tyrant. But the gaudy bird jeered at him no longer. He did not recognize the cat who could climb. Over the last fence and there was the black shape of Mrs Lambert's shed. Sammy peered in and smelt the familiar smell. How often he had slept there. Certainly none of the vagabonds had ever had such a snug shelter, not even Brute. What a pity you could not hang on to the best of both worlds.

There were some frantic squeaks and a scrabbling sound. Sammy's thoughts were miles away. He saw a mouse scurry over the floor. Automatically the big cat froze, his hunter's instinct taking command. The mouse had seen him. Yet it was coming closer. Sammy tensed, ready to pounce.

'Is it Sammy? It can't be. It can't be,' the mouse's shrill voice sounded through the hollow shed. Then something in the cat's pose arrested the little creature and he stopped. He trembled. The next instant he fled as Sammy leapt at him. Squeaks of alarm and protest pulled Sammy up short. Tiptoe! And he could have killed him!

Stella and Josephine were stirring. But Sammy waited no longer. He turned tail before they woke and saw him. How could he come back? He was no longer a pet. He was changed: altered for ever. It had taken a mouse to make him realize it.

Now he ran as swiftly as only he could, leaping at the succeeding fences with impatience. He could think of only one thing. He, Sammy, was now the King Cat. The vagabonds could go where they wished; do what they chose. He wanted only Pinkie and together they would found a new colony of cats in Quartermile Field. One day he would bring them to show Molly. He raced on, across the last garden and into Belinda's meadow. His head was full of thoughts of his future life. The last human dwelling-place was behind him and he sprinted for the road.

From the darkness of the waste ground a small white cat emerged to sit by the roadside. She carefully washed her pink ears and nose as she waited for Sammy, the King of the Vagabonds, to join her.